Caffeine Nights Publishing

The Major Crimes Team

Volume 1

Lines of Enquiry

Graham Smith

Fiction aimed at the heart and
the head...

Published by Caffeine Nights Publishing 2015

CONDITIONS OF SALE

Published in Great Britain by

Caffeine Nights Publishing
4 Eton Close
Walderslade
Chatham
Kent
ME5 9AT

www.caffeine-nights.com

British Library Cataloguing in Publication Data.
A CIP catalogue record for this book is available from the British Library.

ISBN: 978-1-910720-30-1

Cover design by
Mark (Wills) Williams

Everything else by
Default, Luck and Accident

To Helen and Daniel. I could never have achieved this without your support.

Graham Smith is a joiner by trade who has built bridges, dug drains and worked on large construction sites before a career change saw him become the general manager of a busy hotel and wedding venue on the outskirts of Gretna Green. A crime fiction fan from the age of eight, he swaps the romance of weddings for the dark world of crime fiction whenever time allows.

He has been a reviewer for the well respected crime fiction site www.crimesquad.com for four years and has conducted face to face interviews with many stellar names, including Lee Child, David Baldacci, Dennis Lehane, Jeffrey Deaver, Peter James & Val McDermid.

Before turning his hand to novel writing, he was published in several Kindle anthologies including True Brit Grit, Off the Record 2: At the Movies, Action Pulse Pounding Tales: Vol 1 & 2 Graham has three collections of short stories out on Kindle. They are Eleven the Hardest Way (long-listed for a SpineTingler Award), Harry Charters Chronicles and Gutshots: Ten Blows to the Abdomen.

Away from work and crime fiction, Graham enjoys spending time with his wife and son, socialising and watching far too much football.

Recommendations for Graham Smith

Peter James – Author of the Roy Grace series
"...a talented story-teller."

Zoe Sharp –Author of the Charlie Fox novels
".....fast-paced and intriguing. It kept me turning the pages to the end."

Matt Hilton – Author of the Joe Hunter novels
"... Graham Smith is another talent to watch for..."
"... bloody good medicine for the mind."

Richard Godwin – Author of Apostle Rising, Mr Glamour and One Lost Summer
"Smith is a writer with a strong voice who catches the attention and holds it... sharp dialogue and tight plotting..."

Sheila Quigley - Author of The Seahills series and the Holy Island trilogy
"Graham Smith is not just a rising star, but a shooting star."

Joseph Finder - New York Times bestseller
"Smith's anti-hero, Detective Inspector Evans, is the kind of cop we don't see any more, a man more interested in justice than the law. If my children were kidnapped, he's the man I'd want on my side."

Acknowledgements

Without delivering an Oscar style speech, there are an awful lot of people who have helped me to get to this point. From the early writing classes I've attended, the friends I've made both online and in person, the whole community of crime fiction writers have been supportive and have welcomed me into their ranks. Special mentions of course must include Darren Laws of Caffeine Nights who has shown great faith in me, the team behind him, Chris Simmons at Crimesquad.com and Matt Hilton, Michael Malone, Sheila Quigley, Col Bury, David Barber and the whole Crime and Publishment gang for their friendship, advice and unconditional support. My sincerest thanks to you all, I just wish I could find the right words to say how deep my gratitude is.

Graham Smith 2015

Lines of Enquiry

Home Wreckers

Detective Inspector Harry Evans took the call as he was passing Carlisle Crematorium. With practiced dexterity, he spun his BMW M3 in a tight circle and raced towards Levein Grove.

No other crime got his blood pumping the way a murder did. While he never wanted one human being to kill another, it was always exciting when it happened.

Haring between the rows of terraced ex-council houses, he weaved between parked cars only slowing for the ever present speed humps. Ahead of him, he could see a patrol car heading the same way, its strobe lights reflecting off the roughcast walls and up into the night sky.

Determined to arrive before the woodentops had time to trample over any evidence left by the killer, he pressed his right foot hard against the accelerator and rocketed along the concrete street.

It wasn't just a murder case making his blood thrust its way through his veins; it was the name of the victim, a name he'd encountered many times.

Jimmy Watson was a professional miscreant with links to the Leighton family who oversaw most of the organised crime in Cumbria.

His latest task had been orchestrating a series of disturbances, which ended up with home-owners selling their houses at way below market value to the Leighton family. Once a whole terrace had been purchased, the unsavoury occupants would be moved on to another terrace in a different part of town and the Leightons would find new, more respectable tenants for their houses.

To the best of Evans' knowledge, the Leighton family now owned around forty houses in six different terraces. Their own brand of compulsory purchase was effective in making sure they obtained good houses at rock bottom prices.

It was no secret who was behind the chaos, but the Leightons were savvy enough to distance themselves from the trouble. All purchases were done through intermediaries and they had Jimmy Watson acting as their housing manager.

Standing nearer seven feet than six and blessed with the kind of looks a gargoyle would be ashamed of; few homeowners were brave enough to confront him about the tenants he sited next to their homes.

Catching up with the squad car as it pulled up outside Watson's home, Evans hauled on the handbrake and opened his door before the car had fully stopped.

'Get the woodentops to do crowd control then join me in the house. You do the tea and sympathy, I'll do the investigating.'

'Yes, guv.' DC Lauren Phillips set off to do his bidding, blonde hair floating behind her.

Before Evans had a chance to knock on the door, it opened to reveal a spotty teenager whose eyes were red with more than tears. 'You a copper?'

Evans raised his warrant card to the lad's eye level. 'DI Evans.' He knew the teen to be Watson's son, Michael "Mikey" Watson.

While the grief or substances in his veins clouded Mikey's memory, Evans remembered hauling the youth in for petty dealing.

Mikey turned and wandered into the house, so Evans followed him. He could hear the sound of Lauren's heels clacking on the path as she hurried after him.

Entering the house, it was just as he'd expected. Modern décor with traditional flourishes, as both Watson and his wife Kate had their input. Piles of boxes littered much of the available floor space where the Watson boys stored their latest wares.

Trailing Mikey into the lounge, he found a wet-haired Kate sitting in the middle of a leather sofa. Mikey's elder brothers, Dylan and James, sat at either side of their mother with comforting arms and shocked faces.

Mikey's arm extended towards another room, his voice a flat monotone as he spoke. 'Dad's in there. Once we realised he was dead, we kept out.'

Evans shot a glance at Lauren, and opened the door while she stayed with the family.

The prone frame of Jimmy Watson was face down on the kitchen floor. The blood-stained fingers of his left hand reached up towards the fitted cupboards where he'd been trying to raise himself.

A kitchen knife stuck out from his back, the pool of blood beneath him large enough to suggest it had punctured something vital.

Following procedure, Evans stepped forward and tested for a pulse. As expected, he didn't find one.

Pulling his phone from his pocket, he called Control and in a low voice asked for a CSI team to be sent out.

Once the call was made, he stood and looked around the kitchen, taking in the scene with eyes, ears and nose. The oven hummed a quiet whirr beneath the three pans of vegetables resting on the cooker's unlit hobs. A radio tuned to BBC Cumbria gave a muted weather report as the washing machine pressed a pink bra against the transparent window in its door. The smell of fresh blood mixed with the aroma from whatever was in the oven.

Looking around the kitchen, Evans followed the arc of arterial blood which had sprayed from the wound in Watson's back. There was a break in the droplets where his attacker must have blocked its path.

It was a confusing mix for the senses, as domestic normality ran headlong into brutal violence. Despite the levels of domesticity, this was no ordinary family. The Watsons were petty criminals who lived a comfortable life, financed by the misfortune of others.

Their castle being invaded and the slaying of their king was a surprise to Evans. He knew Watson possessed numerous enemies and his passing would be a cause for celebration in many households. Yet these enemies were not the kind of people who dealt in violence. They were the kind of citizens to dial treble nine, write letters to councillors, or sell up and move away.

Confrontation and violence was Watson's domain, yet he was smart enough to never get caught making threats or trading blows on CCTV or anyone's mobile.

Casting his eyes around the room a final time, Evans stepped out of the kitchen and back into the lounge.

A tumbler of amber liquid was held by each of the Watson family. The air in the room carried hints of brandy over the cigarette smoke, the mixed smells almost strong enough to mask the underlying sweet aroma of dope.

Lauren was perched on a stool, making comforting noises underscored with sympathetic questions. Evans saw Mikey's eyes were fixed on Lauren's legs, where her skirt had ridden to mid-thigh. He could tell she was aware of his attention, but was happy to use his distraction to her advantage. The questions she put to him were accompanied with a tender smile.

Evans was pleased at Lauren's progress, but less happy with her tactics. The way she used her femininity to ensnare attention worked, but would one day lead her into trouble either with superiors or defence solicitors. Mikey would tell Lauren anything she wanted to know, as long as he was under the impression he had a chance with her. The fact she was asking about his father and who may have murdered him didn't seem to have registered with Mikey.

The thought was a distracting one, as Evans considered the dynamics of the Watson family.

Mikey was the youngest of Watson's sons and the least likely to stay out of jail. Not blessed with his brothers' sly cunning or his father's imposing bulk, Mikey was the proud owner of two ASBOs and one ankle tag. While initially upset at his father's death, the grief had been parked so he could pursue the attentions of a woman far out of his league, his desperate attempts to please Lauren suggesting a lack of experience with the fairer sex.

'Shut the fuck up Mikey.' Dylan shot his brother a fierce look. 'Dad didn't have any real enemies. Sure, he had a few disagreements with some of the neighbours of the houses he managed. But none of them were ever angry enough to take him on.'

'Are you sure?'

Uncertainty clouded Dylan's eyes as he considered Evans' question.

'There's no one I can think of. But you might want to speak to some of the tenants of the houses he manages ... sorry managed.'

A howl of grief came from Kate when she heard her son change tenses, the correction hammering home the realisation her husband was dead.

A knock at the door interrupted the awkward silence that followed.

Evans rose to his feet. 'I'll get it. It's probably the CSI team.'

Opening the door, he found a woman. Standing a little under five foot, with spiky brown hair and a hard face, the woman was the double of Kate Watson.

Evans stood aside and let her pass. Parked behind his car was a CSI van whose occupants were busy unloading equipment.

Greeting the leader of the team with familiarity, he shared his suspicions and made a few suggestions as to what the CSI team should both expect and look for. A trained Family Liaison Officer followed the CSI team in, so Evans went to retrieve Lauren.

With Watson's family offering forward no suspects, the basis of this investigation would fall into the hands of the CSI geeks. What he had to do now was work his contacts and see who they pointed the finger at, while waiting to see if the CSI team's evidence backed up his hunch.

*   *   *   *

Twenty minutes later, Evans was holding the door of The Green Man open for Lauren. There was no better source of information about Jimmy Watson's enemies than the family who'd helped him create them. The Green Man was the stronghold of the Leighton family, and the place where they held court.

The Green Man was the kind of place where you could buy or sell anything you wanted, as long as you had the good sense not to ask questions. Prostitutes, small-time drug dealers and petty thieves all plied their trade from here. Yet whenever a raid was organised, the Leightons and their customers were always found to be above the law. Evans knew someone must be tipping them off, but he hadn't yet managed to identify their informant.

Adjusting his eyes to the brightly lit interior, Evans clocked Maureen Leighton sitting between her brothers. Dressed as ever in a velour tracksuit, she exuded a quiet confidence, while her brothers scowled at the sight of two coppers walking into their territory.

'Here.' Evans held out a twenty pound note to Lauren. 'Get us a drink and get whatever the Leightons are having.'

As she turned for the bar, he walked across to the Leighton's table, aware of the furtive glances shooting his way. Every one of the patrons was eager to see what was happening. One or two made their way towards the door, as if late for an important appointment.

Evans made a mental note of the early-leavers. These were the ones who had something to hide. A team of woodentops could round them up later and try their luck at getting a conviction or two.

'You got a warrant, copper?' Maureen's restraining hand did little to hold back her brother's ire.

'No, Tony, I haven't. I don't need a warrant to have a conversation.'

'Whatever you want to talk about, we're not saying owt without a brief present.'

'Will you pair keep your gobs shut long enough to see what the bloody hell he wants?' Maureen's frostbitten tone silenced both Dennis and Tony, but didn't erase the antagonism from their faces or body language.

Maureen took a drink from her wine glass and looked at Evans. 'You're here about Jimmy Watson, aren't you?'

'That's right …'

'Well you can forget it, copper. We've been here all day, and have plenty of witnesses to prove it.'

'Dennis, will you either shut up and listen or fuck off.' Maureen glared at her brother. 'If DI Evans was here to arrest us, he'd have come mob-handed. He's here with one female DC, so it stands to reason that all he wants to do is ask a few questions. Harry?'

'You've heard he was found lying on the kitchen floor with a carving knife sticking out of his back, haven't you?'

Maureen nodded. 'I take it you want to know whose hand held the knife?'

'It'd be a help.'

Lauren arrived with the drinks on a dirty plastic tray. As she passed them out, she got a grudged nod thanks from both of Maureen's brothers.

Evans accepted his pint with a smile and pocketed the change without looking at it. Both the Leighton men were looking at Lauren with undisguised longing, despite being old enough to be her father.

Immune to Lauren's charms himself, Evans couldn't help but wonder why she paraded herself with such abandon. Where most female officers went to great lengths to hide their femininity, she used hers as a weapon. Her clothes were always just the right side of decent, but she wasn't averse to using her body to distract suspects and solicitors in interview rooms. He'd witnessed many people get caught out by her piercing questions when distracted by a rising hem or a low neckline.

Tony sprang to his feet and pointed at the door. 'You think we're gonna grass someone up? Fuck off, pig.'

Before Maureen could reprimand her brother, Evans was on his feet looking up at the bigger man. 'Sit down, you imbecile, or I'll sit you down.'

The steel in Evans' voice combined with the fire in his eyes was too much for Tony. Evans' reputation as a fighter was hard earned, and even with his brother to back him up, Tony wasn't prepared to take him on. Yet he could feel the eyes of every customer in The Green Man on him, waiting to see if he was prepared to back down when confronted by a man much smaller than himself.

'I'll sit down when I get back from the bog. Your patter is so shite, I'm in danger of pissing me pants.'

Evans stepped aside and then looked back at Maureen as he took his seat. A look of apology decorated her lined face.

'I know Jimmy Watson was one of your boys, and I'm sure you'll want to do everything you can to make sure his killer is brought to justice.' Evans jabbed a finger onto the table. 'Legal justice.'

'Of course we do. We're deeply saddened by his early passing.'

'Right, then. Who do you know who may have a grudge against him?'

Maureen took a drink of her wine and made a pretence of considering the question, but Evans knew she'd have drawn up her list of suspects within seconds of hearing of Watson's death.

'Peter Nicholson was never a friend of his. He could have had something to do with it.'

'Really? And what makes you think the leader of a rival gang would have anything to do with one of your boys being murdered? I'm not falling for that one, Maureen.'

A shrug. 'Worth a try. That prick's been making a nuisance of himself lately.'

'Cut the bullshit. Tell me who you really think is behind it or I'll whistle up a couple of vans and take you and your brothers down the station.'

'On what basis?'

'Let's just say I suspect you or your brothers killed him because he was stealing from you. If I was to follow that line of enquiry, I'd have to have a team examine all your finances looking for where the money went missing from. Understand?'

Maureen's face took on an indifferent look as she tried to bluff Evans. 'We both know that such an investigation would be a waste of time and resources. Our accounts are above board and Jimmy wasn't stealing from us. Tell me, Harry, how would DCI Grantham and the rest of your superiors feel about another one of your hunches failing to pan out? You'll soon be at the end of your thirty years of service. What then? A support role? Or do you think they'll keep you on to make mistake after mistake?'

'I don't make enough mistakes for them to boot my arse out onto the street. If we take you in and go through your accounts, I'm sure we'll find something to hang you on.'

'Go on, then. Make the call. We'll come quietly.' Maureen held out her arms with her wrists together. 'I warn you, though. Pursuing us when you should be after a killer won't help you. My sources tell me you're already on a sticky wicket. Wasting all that time and money on us will only cover it in glue.'

'Yeah, but if we find something, the credit I'll get for bringing you down will make me untouchable.'

'Roll the dice, Harry. I'm game if you are.'

The confident way her eyes never left his was un-nerving. She was calling his bluff big time. And that's all it was from him, a bluff. He didn't for one minute think the Leightons' accounts would show anything other than what they were supposed to show.

Lauren came to his rescue. 'Say we do bring you in and it turns out to be the waste of time you suggest. Do you think your business will be unscathed in the time we're looking into it and you? It's no secret Peter Nicholson is desperate to get his hands on some of your territory. I'm sure he'll jump at the chance. And you've no idea how slow some of our accounting guys are. They could take weeks, months even, to go through everything of yours.'

Maureen's eyes narrowed to slits as Lauren's words hit their intended target. The Leightons had taken years to reach the pinnacle of organised crime in Cumbria, and had seen off many pretenders to their throne along the way. Yet Maureen was more aware than most to the dangers of bleeding in shark-infested water.

Time spent dealing with Evans' faux enquiry would distract her attention from the day-to-day running of her many businesses. Something, somewhere, would slip, and Peter Nicholson or another rival would pounce. They may be able to reclaim their lost assets, but it would take time and money to do so.

'Let's all cut the bullshit. Jimmy wasn't under threat from anyone. Perhaps a few folk who lived next to the houses he managed tenants for weren't happy with him, but I can't see them sticking a knife in his back.' A hesitation as she weighed up the consequences of her next words. 'You know Jimmy was a player, right?'

Evans nodded. 'So I've heard. But I thought he'd knocked it on the head after the last time Kate found out. Beats me how that ugly bugger was ever a player, though.'

'Women are interested in more than looks. Jimmy had a real charm about him when he wanted something.' A wistful smiled crossed Maureen's lips. 'He didn't stop; he just got better at covering his tracks. Kate taking the boys to her sister's gave him a real wake-up call. It took him weeks to sweet-talk her into coming back, but he didn't change his ways.'

'So, who's he been sleeping with?'

'He was seeing a lass from Kendal on a regular basis.' Maureen looked at Dennis. 'What's her name?'

Concentration drifted across Dennis' already bleary eyes as he trawled his memory for a name. 'Susan something or other. He didn't talk about her much, but I know he met her at the Crown.'

'Does she live in the area?' Lauren accompanied her question with a smile and a slight lean forward.

Dennis' eyes found her intended target and locked on. 'Yeah, she's got her own place in the town, but I don't know where.'

'Was he seeing anyone else?'

'Not on a regular basis, but he'd shag a working girl anytime he got a spare few quid his wife didn't know about.'

'I think that answers all your questions, Harry.' Maureen's tone was pointed. 'Unless you want to make a fool of yourself.'

'You called my bluff and I folded. Don't be the kind of bitch who milks it.'

'A bitch? Me? Surely you're thinking of someone else.' Maureen's laugh was natural and girlish, despite her advancing years. 'I hear your Janet's in the family way. Congratulations.'

'Thanks.' Evans couldn't keep the smile from his face. He'd never expected to become a father, but when Janet had told him she was pregnant, he'd realised just how much he wanted a child.

*   *   *   *

Back in his beloved M3, Evans sped along London Road towards the M6 while Lauren put in a call to DS Neil Chisholm. The obese sergeant was a computer geek who could illicit all kinds of information from the internet that wasn't held on the Police National Database.

Waiting until Lauren finished her call, Evans concentrated on getting to the motorway as quickly as possible. It was getting too late to go knocking on doors. The later you disturbed the public, the less inclined they were to help you.

Thumbing the controls on the steering wheel, he selected a number and put in a call to Will Cuthbertson, the DI at Kendal.

'Will, it's the He-Man. I'm coming down your way and need to pick your brains.'

A disembodied voice popped out of the car's speakers. 'Al'right, Harry, what do you need to know?'

'You know the Crown on Junction Street? Owned by the Leightons?'

'Aye. What about it?'

'Do you know of a Susan who works there, or is a regular, or anything like that?'

A weary sigh came through the speakers before Cuthbertson answered. 'Not that I can think of. There's a Suzanne Thomas, runs the Drake at Windermere, but I don't know of anyone called Susan who works at the Crown.'

'No bother. Thanks anyroad.'

Evans hung up and corrected a slide as the BMW's powerful rear-wheel drive pushed the back end of the car out as he sped round the roundabout.

'What's your thoughts on this, guv?'

'I think the answer is connected to his flies. Money is out the question. Big as he was, Watson wasn't stupid enough to steal from them, and he's making plenty of money from them. His house showed as much.'

'If you're right about that, it puts the wife in the frame. Or one of the boys getting angry with him for hurting their mum for a second time.'

'Possible. But which one of the four, and how would you prove it when the other three will provide alibis for them?'

'Fair point. What about revenge?'

'Doesn't seem likely. If anyone had a grudge against him, then it had to be someone brave enough to take on the Leightons as well. That hasn't happened, and you can be sure we just interrupted a council of war.'

Lauren pursed her lips. 'If someone was making a play for the Leightons' territory, wouldn't it be wise to take him out early?'

'It would.' Evans flashed a quick glance at her. 'How many gangland murders have you heard of where the victim is stabbed in the back in his own kitchen?'

'None. But by the same token, it could have been done that way to disguise the killer's real target. By taking him out, the Leightons are either going to have to start looking after those tenants themselves, or find someone else to do it. I dunno about you, but I can't think of anyone else in their gang who could fill his shoes.'

Lauren had made a fair point about the fact a rival may have disguised their intentions. Watson's murder could be the beginning of a bloody turf war. With The Green Man as the headquarters of the Leighton empire, it was a logical target, but Evans doubted anyone would be brave enough to take on the Leightons there. Any direct attacks on them would be more likely to happen when they were divided. Killing Watson was a direct way to divide them, as Tony or Dennis would have to step into Watson's role until a suitable replacement was anointed.

Am I jumping at shadows here, or should I put some kind of discreet surveillance in place? It'd be nice to see them taken down, but a turf war is bad news for everyone.

'Say that is the case, Lauren. Who would you point the finger at? Peter Nicholson isn't yet strong enough to take them on in an open war, and he's the closest to the Leightons in terms of size and manpower.'

'Who says it has to be someone local? What if it's a firm from Newcastle, Glasgow or Manchester looking to expand their operations? The Leightons might be big cheeses around here, but they're small fry in real terms.'

Evans shook his head. 'If it was a firm from elsewhere, we'd be investigating the murders or disappearances of the entire Leighton family. Big fish don't nibble a little fish's fins, they eat them whole.'

'Oh.' Lauren's head dipped forward a little. 'So that's why you think sex is behind it.'

Evans said nothing. He was interested in seeing what Lauren's thoughts were. When you got past the pretty face and blatant exhibitionism, she had a sharp mind.

'If you think it's sex-related, why aren't you speaking to the wife and the boys when they are still consumed with grief?'

'You've got until we get to Kendal before you have to answer your own question.'

Evans powered past a lumbering wagon and rounded a corner at such a pace, he could feel all four wheels begin to drift. Correcting the drift with a touch of over-steer, he buried his right foot to the floor and thundered towards the next bend, unheeding of the treacherous conditions.

'I've got it.' Lauren's voice tinkled with confidence.

'I'll drop you at the clinic. They'll give you some penicillin.'

'Very funny. Shall I see if they've got a cure for male pattern baldness when I'm there?' Lauren was used to Evans' barbed jokes about her sex life, and knew the best way to deal with him was to give as good as she took. 'You don't think it's the wife or one of the boys. You think it's the husband or boyfriend of whoever he was knocking off?'

'Well done. I'll phone your mother and tell her to put an extra tattie on your plate as reward for your excellent deduction.'

Evans pulled out to overtake a slow moving Mondeo as Lauren searched in her handbag. 'You're such a wit. Or at least half a … Jesus Christ, guv.' Evans managed to get the BMW back into the left-hand lane before the oncoming van hit them, but it was a close thing.

'Want one?' Evans lit a cigarette and powered his window down an inch. Drops of rain, blown through the window by the turbulent air, splattered the side of his face.

The near miss had been closer than he'd cared for. He knew Janet worried about his high-speed driving. Now she was pregnant, she refused to travel with him unless he promised to stick to the speed limits and avoid taking unnecessary risks.

Lauren pulled her phone out and called Chisholm again. Listening with the mobile jammed between ear and shoulder, she jotted a few lines into her notebook.

*   *   *   *

Chisholm had come through in spades for them. He'd managed to identify all the staff of The Crown by going through PAYE submissions. Finding no Susan listed as a Christian or middle name, he'd expanded his search to include family members of the full-time staff.

The manageress had a married sister called Susan Galbraith. Checking her name against the Electoral Register, he'd got her address and other details. She was the right age, her husband was a Sergeant Major in the Marines, and she was the only Susan he'd found with a connection to The Crown.

Chisholm had also given Lauren the addresses of three other Susans who lived in Kendal, but this seemed the most promising.

Evans parked on Greengate Lane and clambered out. Knocking on doors after ten o'clock on a Tuesday night in a respectable area would see them met with anger or fear for a family member's health.

Looking along the street, he saw most houses had their downstairs lights off. One or two had upstairs lights on where people would be reading or preparing for bed. The inhabitants of a street like this would all have work or school runs to cope with in the morning. Suburban life had its own timescales, and Greengate Lane was the kind of place where every occupant would contribute to society.

'C'mon then. Showtime.'

Walking past the immaculate garden, Evans pressed the doorbell and waited. Getting no answer, he pressed again.

He heard the chimes, but again there was no reaction.

Evans rapped his knuckles on the door. Hard.

Is she a deep sleeper? Has she wrapped herself around a decent bottle of wine before bedtime? Is she out with another lover?

Taking a few steps back, he looked for signs of life inside the house. There were none.

From the corner of his eye, he could see Lauren pressing her mobile against her ear. She waved him over.

'When you didn't get an answer, I got DS Chisholm to track her mobile. He says it hasn't moved from here since teatime yesterday.'

'Shite.'

Either Susan was comatose inside the house, or she'd gone out without her mobile. Knowing how few people left home without their phones, Evans had a sinking feeling about being able to raise Susan.

Every minute of Evans' thirty years' experience was telling him something was off. The house was in darkness, yet the curtains weren't drawn. There was a car in the driveway, but the house seemed deserted. If Susan had gone out, she'd done so on foot and without her mobile.

Turning his collar up against the all-encompassing drizzle, Evans trudged towards a gate leading to the back of the house.

Stepping through the gate, he found a narrow passage leading to the back of the house. A wheelie-bin was backed up against the house wall, the house's number hand-painted onto its front as a mark of identification.

Reaching the back of the house, Evans found a rear door overlooking the garden. Looking up, he saw the back of the house was also in darkness.

'Shall I try the door?' Lauren reached out a hand.

'Gloves!'

Lauren's eyebrows arched as she caught the significance of Evans' instruction. 'You think there's something wrong?'

'I dunno about wrong, but summat's not right.'

Grabbing the handle with a gloved hand, Lauren tried the door. It opened.

Evans touched her shoulder and intimated she let him go first. The gesture earned him a scowl.

'I'm a trained officer.'

'And I'm an inspector. Step aside.' Evans pulled out his collapsible baton, flicking his wrist to extend it.

Pushing the door open with the tip of his baton, he glanced left and right before stepping into the kitchen. 'Hello. Anybody home?' He'd learned the hard way never to enter a house without announcing his presence. When confronted by a stranger in their house, home-owners were liable to hit first and ask questions second, especially late at night.

No answer came back to him. Nor any sounds of movement.

Flicking on the light, he let his eyes dance round the room, taking in the modern fittings and expensive gadgets as they searched for possible aggressors.

Opening the first door he came to, he found a dining room. Six chairs surrounded a mahogany table, and a matching dresser stood against the far wall. A large montage depicted a poodle-permed blonde accompanied by a man and a boy. The pictures charted the various stages of the boy's life, with the most recent picture showing him dressed in the robes and mortarboard of a university passing out ceremony. The man in the pictures was the same man and, in at least half of them, he wore a military uniform.

Again there was no life to be found in the room.

Evans moved on to the next door and switched on the light. It was the lounge and, just like the previous rooms, the furniture and décor was modern and expensive.

Evans looked at Lauren, who shrugged. 'She's either upstairs or she's gone out.'

'Wow, that's clever of you. You should be a detective.'

Calling out as he went, Evans made his way into the hallway and up the stairs. Reaching the landing at the top, he peered through three open doors to find un-occupied bedrooms.

That left the bathroom.

Evans banged on the door. 'Susan. It's the police. Are you in there?'

No answer. He looked at Lauren, reluctant to enter a woman's bathroom when she may be lying in a state of drunken undress.

Her eyes rolled. '*Now* you want me to go first.'

Grasping the door handle, she teased the door open and reached for the pull cord. When the light came on, Lauren and Evans gasped in unison.

A blonde woman lay in an empty bath, wearing nothing but a cerise thong. It wasn't her nudity which made them gasp. It was the ruined mess of her chest. To Evans' eye, it looked as if she'd been attacked by a demented butcher.

Slash marks and stab wounds decorated her entire upper torso. Evans checked for a pulse, knowing he was wasting his time. There was no way anyone could have survived the wounds on this woman's chest.

'You call Control. I'll take some pictures.'

Evans used his iPhone to capture a number of pictures of the woman in her final resting place. The CSI team would document everything properly, but he wanted to get a few images to have at his disposal right away.

Once he'd got the pictures, he made a call of his own. Questions were asked and answers given. A minute later he hung up and made enquiries of another source. Getting the information he wanted, Evans made a third call. The final one was short and to the point. Instead of asking questions he gave orders.

* * * *

It was well after midnight when Evans and Lauren were able to hand the investigation over to the CSI team. Will Cuthbertson had turned up wanting to help out, but Evans had used his position in Major Crimes to pull rank and keep the investigation as his own.

There had been numerous emergency services arriving at the house, and their presence had kept both Lauren and Evans occupied as protocols were observed and procedures followed.

Now that they were back in the car and returning to Carlisle, he had a chance to tell her of the arrest he'd made.

'Kate Watson.' Lauren lit a menthol cigarette. 'Why do you reckon it's her?'

'A few reasons.'

'C'mon, guv. Don't start pretending you're shy. I know you better than that.'

'Watson had a knife in his back. Therefore whoever stabbed him got the jump on him from behind in his own home. To me, that suggests either a surprise intruder or someone he felt confident of turning his back on. The tea was all set to be made, which means Kate was about. Which in turn means nobody could have got the jump on him. When I looked at where he'd been attacked, there was a spray of blood on the wall. The spray of blood had a gap in it. The gap was roughly human-sized. Ergo the attacker was sprayed by the victim's blood.'

'Kate Watson told me she was in the shower when the boys came home and found him.'

'I guessed as much. Her hair was wet, but she'd been cooking tea, and she hadn't been out in the rain as her clothes were dry.'

'That's not enough to suspect someone of murder.' Lauren ground the butt of her cigarette into the overflowing ashtray.

'If you'd stop fucking interrupting me, I'd be able to tell you it all.' Evans stopped talking to Lauren so he could berate a driver who had the temerity to observe the speed limits.

'What else, guv?'

'She was already on my suspect list by then, so I got the CSI guys to check the shower drain to see if there were any traces of Watson's blood in there. There was.' Evans lit a cigarette from the butt of the one he was smoking. 'The washing machine was on, so I also got them to check the laundry basket for women's clothes. It was empty, which meant she must have stripped off before going upstairs for her shower. It's circumstantial, but it was enough to make me pay attention to her.'

'Wow!'

Evans drove in silence for a few minutes, as Lauren digested his logic. He knew she'd be chastising herself for not picking up on some of the clues. He didn't like to gloat of his successful hunches paying off, but he did feel his logic processes should be passed onto the junior members of the team.

'I can see why you fancy her for Watson's murder, but what about Susan Galbraith's? Doesn't the husband come into it?'

'I had Chisholm check out his whereabouts as soon as I heard the husband was in the Marines. He's been in Afghanistan for the last two months and is due home in a fortnight. Chisholm also checked Kate Watson's number plate against the ANPR records. Her car was recorded as entering Kendal at ten fifteen last night and leaving a half-hour later. To cap it off, she picked up a speeding ticket at the bottom of Greengate Lane as she left. That puts her in the vicinity of a murder victim whom she has a motive to kill. Add the damage done to the victim by her attacker, and you get the picture of a deranged murderer. Susan Galbraith wasn't killed cleanly by an expert. She was murdered by someone who'd lost touch with reality. I'll bet you a week's wages and a night of passion with the chief constable that a lot of her wounds will have been inflicted after she died.'

*　　*　　*　　*

Evans got back to his flat at half-past six, just as the first rays of sunlight were appearing. Kate Watson had tried stonewalling at first, but when confronted with all the evidence, her defence had crumbled. After that, it had been a case of charging her and filling in the endless forms.

He planned to get a few hours sleep and then take Janet out for the day. This was one of those rare occasions when their respective shifts granted them a chance to spend time together without either of them being on call or due to start work later in the day. Her work as an Accident and Emergency Surgeon at Cumbria Infirmary and his career in the police always seemed to conspire against them.

Creeping into the living room, he heard a gentle sob. He opened the door to their bedroom to be greeted by darkness.

'Harry?' The grief in Janet's voice broke his heart.

'What is it, darling?'

Evans switched on the light and found Janet lying on the floor. Her arms were wrapped around their three-legged Labrador, her beautiful face distorted and tear-stained.

Kneeling beside Janet and releasing her arms from Tripod, he pulled her into a tender embrace. 'What is it? What's wrong? Are you OK?'

Her body convulsed in his arms as great wracking sobs shook her body. When she was able to speak, her words were a whisper in his ear. 'I'm so sorry. So very sorry.'

He knew then what she was going to say. He'd thought perhaps her mother or a close friend had died suddenly. That wasn't the case.

Realisation of their loss stole his breath. Dried his mouth to a crisp. Attempts to provide comfort failed, as the words just wouldn't come. The urge to squeeze her tight had to be contained lest he crush the life from her in his shared grief.

'Are you sure?' He knew the futility of his question. As a woman, she'd know, and as a surgeon, she'd recognise all the symptoms of miscarriage. He just didn't want it to be true.

Neither of them had expected her to fall pregnant, but when she'd told him she was expecting, it was the happiest day of his life.

Manhunters

DS Neil Chisholm pushed back his chair and eased his bulk upright. It had been a quiet week, so he'd spent his spare time perfecting a new surveillance algorithm.

Designed to flag up any specific trigger-words used on social media, the algorithm was similar to ones used by international espionage agencies. Chisholm had added a few tweaks and parameters to his, though.

First, it was contained to only monitoring accounts registered to addresses in Cumbria. Second, it would also pick up visitors to the area using smart-phones to connect to social media outlets like Facebook, Twitter and Pinterest. Once the visitors went outside the county, they would be dropped from the database, unless they had activated a trigger.

He'd chosen his trigger words and phrases with care. Knowing the public's dislike of proper grammar on social media sites, he'd included as many common misspellings as he could think of.

Also included in his algorithm's remit were various instant messaging sites and apps.

The algorithm had been doing its thing for a few days now. He'd had a regular stream of alerts, but so far none of them were worth pursuing.

He knew what he was doing was illegal, but he was confident his algorithm would never be detected. If it bore fruit, he knew his boss – DI Harry Evans – would help him keep the algorithm a secret from the brass.

His love of computers, and a natural aptitude at programming, saw him pretty-much desk-bound at all times, but he wouldn't have it any other way. Sure, he missed the excitement of the chase, but he didn't miss being lied to, spat at and assaulted. He got his job satisfaction from providing Evans and the rest of the Major Crimes team with the information they needed to solve their cases.

Returning from the toilet, he sat down and opened the bottom drawer of his desk. No files, documents or stationery had ever been in this drawer. The drawer contained his stash of chocolate bars and energy drinks.

Evans strode into the room as Chisholm was dropping a wrapper onto the overflowing pile that was his waste bin.

'Got anything for us, Jabba?'

Chisholm wasn't offended by Evans' nickname for him. He'd heard far worse, and knew Evans wouldn't allow anyone else to insult him. Considering the loss his DI had just suffered, he was surprised to see him at work.

'Nothing that'd interest you, guv. There's a dubious fire at a house in Maryport, a spate of shoplifting at Penrith, and few muggings in Kendal.'

'They're hardly major crimes. Are there no heists or murders to investigate?'

'Nothing like that.'

Evans scratched the top of his bald head. 'Anyone hurt in the fire?'

'No, but they had to evacuate half the street.'

'Fuck it. I'll go and take a look at it. There's nowt else interesting.' Evans pointed a finger at DC Amir Bhaki. 'You go to Penrith and get the crack on the shoplifting. I'll pick up Lauren and take her with me.'

'What about the muggings?'

'Too easy. Barry Hammond got out of jail last week. A fiver says Will Cuthbertson will already have him in custody.'

Chisholm knew better than to wager against one of Evans' hunches. They were so legendary in the station, he'd been christened Quasi by all those brave enough to use the term to his face.

* * * *

The rest of Chisholm's afternoon passed without any notable events, until an alert came in from his algorithm. Checking it out, he found someone had created a new Facebook group called '*Cumbria Against PAEDOS*', the capitalisation of paedos a red flag in itself.

Logging onto the site with one of several profiles he'd created, he looked at the group the way a typical user would see it. Nothing too hateful was obvious, but there was an underlying current of anger in the group description. Reading down the list of members, he recognised a few names from the more volatile elements of society.

There was no administrator listed for the group, so Chisholm opened another window on his screen and went into Facebook via the algorithm. Five minutes later, he'd tracked down the administrator.

Garry Robertson was a well-known figure to Cumbria Constabulary. Any time there was any kind of major disturbance or protest, he was involved. Too clever to get his own hands dirty, Robertson was an inciter and provoker who specialised in creating ammunition for others to fire. Never convicted of an actual crime, he'd been present at many incidents. His presence was always a background one, with his arms wound around a distraught relative or used to restrain a late-arriving aggressor.

Ever-present but never ostensibly involved, he was known to cause more problems than he solved.

Minimising the second window, Chisholm used his fake profile to request membership of the group. The profile he'd chosen was one he'd set up to make himself look like a bigoted nationalist. He'd already managed to hook up with a few like-minded morons. By engaging with them, he'd established himself as just the kind of person Robertson could enlist to do his own dirty work.

Twenty-five minutes later, he'd been accepted into the group and had received a friend request from Robertson.

Scrolling down the page, he read message after message from members who had pledged their support to the group. Ten or twenty had gone so far as to allege paedophilia upon their neighbours or someone they'd seen outside the school. In the time it took to read to the bottom of the comment stream, another ten members had been added.

A new post grabbed Chisholm's attention.

Troy Joserand lives on Orton Road. He's a pedo whose been relocated by the council after he got out ov jail. We should drive him out. Now!

The poster had no profile picture and went under the name Paedos Beware. Likes poured in for the comment as other members agreed Joserand should be removed from the community. Some even pledged their support and suggested a meeting place.

Chisholm watched as people signed up to the idea of driving him out. The original poster added a new thread to the group.

I say we give the bastard a good kicking. Thoughts?

The replies streamed in, suggesting everything from a stern warning to burning the house down and castrating him with a pair of rusty scissors.

Chisholm put on a pair of headphones and called Evans as he tapped at his keyboard to learn the true identity of the poster known as Paedos Beware.

'Guv, you're not gonna believe this but I've managed to discover a planned vigilante attack … via Facebook … Of course it's not legal, but that's not important right now … Their intended victim is called Troy Joserand and lives in Carlisle. They're planning to attack him at nine tonight. What should we do about it?'

Chisholm listened to Evans' answer, then ended the call.

Following Evans' instruction, he called Control and warned them to be aware of false 999 calls directing police forces to the opposite end of town at 9pm.

Next, he finished tracing Paedos Beware, only to discover Garry Robertson was the presence behind it with a secondary account.

Evans had also tasked him with finding out more about Troy Joserand, as the name was unfamiliar to them both.

Starting at the beginning, he checked the Police National Database, but turned up a blank. Next, he checked the social services and prison system databases. Neither of them had any details of a Troy Joserand.

Chisholm was glad he wasn't searching for a Bill Jones or a John Armstrong. The name Troy Joserand wasn't a common one, which made his search easier. It was, however, so unique, it started to ring a few alarm bells of its own.

What if his name isn't really Troy Joserand? What if that's a pseudonym or a name given to him by someone else?

As the thoughts ran through Chisholm's brain, he came to the realisation that if Troy Joserand was indeed an alias, the only people who could have placed him in a council-owned property were the Protected Witness Scheme.

Experience had taught him the Protected Witness Scheme didn't have a readily accessible database. For security reasons, they didn't have a central database connected to computers with internet access.

That left him with only one alternative.

*   *   *   *

Evans walked back towards his M3, with Lauren at his heels. The cause of the fire had been identified with ease by the senior fire officer.

The owner of the house had been growing cannabis plants in his attic and one of the heat lights had fused, starting the fire. Everyone attending the scene, apart from the firemen wearing breathing apparatus, displayed the effects of the burnt cannabis. Nobody felt any urgency and a few of the bystanders had dissolved into fits of giggles.

Fighting to keep his temper somewhere close to acceptable, he struggled through the crowd, fishing in his pocket to retrieve his mobile. Despite the fire now being extinguished, people were still turning up to gawp at the ruined house. He guessed a significant amount of them were after a free high.

'What?'

Evans listened as Chisholm relayed his suspicions about Troy Joserand.

Making sure nobody could overhear him, Evans gave a series of instructions and hung up.

Sending Lauren on an imaginary errand to get rid of her for a few minutes, he climbed into his car and called his old friend, ACC Greg Hadley.

If Troy Joserand was a protected witness, the ACC would know about him. That kind of information was on a need to know basis and, as a DI, he wasn't deemed worthy of the knowledge.

* * * *

Chisholm munched on another chocolate bar while he watched the comments pour in. Everyone commenting on the thread was condemning Joserand for his alleged paedophilia, and an ever growing number were agreeing to meet at the specified place.

His phone was answered before the first ring was complete. He didn't get a chance to speak, as Evans bombarded him with information.

When he did open his mouth, it was to make a suggestion. He'd been thinking about the best way to handle the assembling lynch mob and had come up with an idea.

Evans gave him the green light, so he started putting his plan into action.

First, he put a call into Control. They argued with his request for two dozen riot-equipped constables and six vans. It was only when he explained what he needed them for that he got his way.

Second, he added two more of his fake profiles to the Facebook group. He didn't think his original one would be cut out of the group, but if it was, he wanted to maintain a presence in there.

While he was doing this, he called the Witness Protection Scheme and, using a reference number supplied by ACC Hadley, got a physical description of Troy Joserand and a contact number for him.

Evans hadn't given him many details, but he'd intimated that Joserand wasn't the usual kind of toe-rag who gave up others to lessen their own sentence. If this was true, Joserand must be in the scheme because he was a witness to a major crime.

Whatever else happened tonight, Joserand mustn't be harmed.

Using his own mobile, he sent a text to Joserand's mobile to identify himself and offer support.

His plan was simple enough, provided everyone played their parts as directed. A half hour before the mob was due to meet, Joserand was to leave his home and make his way to the small shop near the junction with Dobinson Road. He'd be collected there and taken to a safe place.

Then, Chisholm would close the net on his would-be attackers. With luck, there would be a decent number of the less desirable elements of society caught in this trap.

Everything about his plan hinged on collecting Joserand and spiriting him away before the mob found out he was gone. If anything went wrong, he would be serving Joserand up on a plate.

*   *   *   *

The man known as Troy Joserand shut the bathroom door and bent over the toilet. The call he'd just had from his probation officer had gone through him quicker than a dodgy kebab.

Vomiting until there was nothing left to come but thin streams of bile, he straightened himself and brushed his teeth.

A text had come in from someone identifying himself as DS Chisholm. The text urged him to answer the phone if this number called it. He would have doubted the provenance of the text had he not been forewarned of it by the probation officer acting as his handler.

Why the bloody hell did I step forward and give a description of those men? Why couldn't I keep my big mouth shut and turn a blind eye?

He knew the answer to this question. He'd asked it often enough. His mouth had been opened because he'd witnessed a gang of five youths haul someone out of a car and slash his throat.

The attack had happened as he'd been walking back to his car after a night out in his native Liverpool. The five aggressors had jumped into the back of a van and sped off. While he waited for the ambulance to come, he'd told the operator everything he'd seen, including the registration of the van.

The van had been stopped and all its occupants arrested. He'd later been told their victim was a small-time dealer affiliated with a rival gang. He'd been relocated to Carlisle, as a precaution, after he'd agreed to testify in court.

Some bloody precaution. Now the locals want to kill me too!

Going to the bedroom, he replaced jeans and shirt with gym clothes. While it may not keep the evening chill away, it would allow him freedom of movement if he had to run for it.

For ten minutes, he went through a series of stretches. He didn't believe he'd need to run for it, but if he had to, he didn't want to pull a muscle. That would be the equivalent of handing himself over.

Pulling a dark hoodie on over his thin T-shirt, he slipped his phone and wallet into the front pocket.

Flitting his eyes up and down the street, he found no possible aggressors, so he broke into a jog, more to warm his muscles than to get to the shop quicker.

Not feeling safe in the house, he'd left earlier than he'd needed to. If necessary, he could sprint down to the big junction where Orton Road joined Wigton Road. There was a chip shop and another small store that would still be open. Plus there was always traffic on Wigton Road. While bystanders may or may not save him, he knew their presence should inhibit any assailants.

He'd witnessed an attack but, in that instance, the attackers were fuelled by gang loyalty and had not known he was watching. Tonight, the attackers would be fuelled by beer and a righteous, if misplaced, indignation at perceived crimes.

*   *   *   *

Evans screeched to a halt behind an Astra and pounded the steering wheel with the heel of his fist.

'Fuck's sake. Why does this have to happen right in front of us?'

Lauren ignored the question and leapt out of the car and started running towards the accident.

Getting there, she found an articulated lorry jack-knifed across the road, the front end halfway through a hedge while the trailer blocked both lanes of the A595.

The way the cab was at right angles to the trailer meant there was no way the lorry could free itself. It would have to be pulled free by a tow-truck. The smell of diesel in the air, suggesting the fuel tank had been ruptured, just complicated matters further.

If they did manage to somehow get the lorry moved, there was no way they could leave the scene before Traffic arrived.

'What happened?' She held her warrant card up to the wagon driver's window.

'Bloody boy racers overtook me on a blind bend. I had to slam on the anchors so they didn't run into that car.'

Lauren followed his finger. A Citroen was lodged tight up against the side of the lorry's cab. A man in his mid-sixties stood against the Citroen, pale faced and breathing heavily.

Turning at the sound of an insistent horn, Lauren saw Evans had turned his car around and reversed down the westbound carriageway.

'Anybody hurt?'

Lauren took another look at the Citroen driver. 'No, guv.'

'Get in then. I've called it in. Traffic'll be here in five or ten minutes. They can deal with it.'

Lauren hadn't even shut the car door when Evans screeched off in search of an alternate route.

Evans slammed through a gear change. 'Call Jabba. Tell him we're gonna be late.'

*   *   *   *

Chisholm took Lauren's phonecall with a sense of growing dread. Before she'd even hung up, he was reaching for his mobile.

'Troy? It's DS Chisholm. The car coming to collect you has been slightly delayed … No, it should be there in about fifteen minutes. Stay put and we'll have someone there as soon as possible. Call me if you need to move.'

With ten minutes to go before the appointed meeting time, he decided there was time to wait for Evans and Lauren to collect Joserand. The vigilantes may not make their move until they'd had a few pints to embolden themselves. He needed to be here to co-ordinate everything and couldn't go riding off to the rescue. If he left his post, the vigilantes couldn't be led into his trap.

Just as he made this decision, a new comment on Facebook changed his mind altogether.

Just seen him. He's in the paki shop. Will follow him to see where he goes.

*   *   *   *

Joserand pressed the phone against his ear and tried to follow the instructions DS Chisholm was giving him. While the voice on the end of the phone was comforting, and giving what seemed like good advice, it was a different matter for him to hear it.

Pretending to be talking to a family member, he willed himself not to turn and look at the woman eyeing him with disgust as she typed into her mobile. Instead, he did as instructed and browsed a magazine or two, before using the reflection in a window to identify his follower.

It was a chubby woman, whose hair was scraped back into a ponytail so tight, it doubled as a facelift. She was a familiar face on the street, and he knew she lived four doors along from the house he'd been put in. She spent most of her days shouting at her kids or pushing a double buggy back and forth. Tracksuits and slogan-bearing t-shirts were her clothes of choice, each item straining at the seams as it tried to contain her glutinous bulk. A mobile phone was always clutched, by meaty fingers, as if it were a winning lottery ticket.

Eager to leave the shop as soon as possible, Joserand turned for the door. He half considered grabbing her mobile to deprive her of her means of communication, but he thought better of it. He wasn't a thief and there was no way he was going to give her any possible reason to further brand him.

As he walked from the shop, he sent a text to Chisholm, informing him, as instructed, which way he was going and a description of the clothes he wore.

The thud of heavy footsteps sounded in his ears as she tried to keep pace with him. He lengthened his stride, but did not start to run or jog lest she call in reinforcements.

Following Chisholm's suggestion, he made his way towards Wigton Road, towards bystanders, towards witnesses.

The hoodie he wore was a double-edged sword. While hiding his identity, it also restricted his peripheral vision, preventing him from seeing any potential attackers. Aware of the chubby woman following him, he dropped the hood down his back and used his increased vision to scan the road ahead. Chisholm had told him to watch for a red M3 'driven aggressively by an angry bald man'.

*   *   *   *

Lauren stayed quiet as Evans ranted about the slow-moving car in front of them. The country lanes they'd been forced onto afforded no overtaking opportunities. The driver of the car in front wasn't in any hurry, and the way they drove with exaggerated care made Lauren suspect they'd been drinking.

Evans' phone rang, so he hit a button on the steering wheel. The display in the central console showed Janet's name.

'Hello. Is that Harry Evans?' The female voice was unfamiliar to Lauren, who felt her heart sink.

'Yes. Who're you, and why are you calling from my wife's phone?'

'It's Dr McAdam. I work with your wife.'

'Is she OK?'

'She's going to be fine.' There was a measured calmness about Dr McAdam's voice. 'She collapsed with a raging infection. We've got her prepped for surgery, and she'll be going down to theatre in a few minutes.'

'Surgery? What are you doing to her?' The panicked stress in Evans' voice made Lauren wince in sympathy for him. Evans had tried to carry on as normal since Janet had lost their baby, but his brave face had slipped from time to time, while the team had had to tolerate him being even more irritable than usual.

'She needs an emergency hysterectomy. Don't worry, she'll be fine.'

'I'll be there as soon as I can. Fifteen minutes tops.'

The car in front turned off, allowing Evans to bury his right foot to the floor.

'You okay, guv?'

'I'm Harry Evans. The He-Man. Of course I'm o-fucking-kay.' Evans' aggravated tone exposed the lies of his words.

'If you're going to the hospital, shall I call Chisholm so he can have someone else collect Joserand?'

'No need. There's enough time for me to get to the hospital and then you to take the car and pick him up. The more people we bring in on this, the more chance there is of Jabba being fired.'

'OK.'

Lauren was well aware of Evans' loyalty to his team, but the way he still managed to think of Chisholm's career, while worrying about his wife, showed the decency he kept hidden underneath his brash exterior.

As Evans drove, Lauren tapped out a message to Chisholm, informing him of the change in plans.

*　*　*　*

Chisholm read Lauren's text with a mixture of concern and exasperation. Evans and his wife were still reeling from the loss of their baby and didn't need any further upset. But the news that Lauren would be delayed from collecting Joserand by at least another five minutes threw his plans into jeopardy.

Picking up his mobile, he called Joserand and gave him a terse series of instructions. His next call was made to the fourth member of the team.

Amir Bhaki picked up after the fourth ring, his voice muffled as he chewed on something.

'Amir, it's DS Chisholm. We've got a situation and I need your help.'

Chisholm listened to the young DC give his assent and then bombarded him with a concise update, followed by directions to where Joserand would be.

When he checked Facebook again, the latest post made his blood run cold.

The only positive he could take from the situation was that the vigilante group didn't know their moves were being watched.

His instructions to Joserand had pre-empted this situation, albeit for different reasons.

All he could do now was wait to see what unfolded. If Joserand managed to slip his tail, he could be picked up by either Bhaki or Lauren and the vigilantes could be rounded up as planned.

Yet if they got too close to him, he'd have to call in the teams of riot-prepared constables and kiss his career goodbye.

Losing his job wouldn't be a problem financially, as he knew his computer skills were more than good enough to get him a better-paid job in a matter of days. What would grieve him would be the lack of making a difference.

Not being on the front line of policing, he didn't see the eyes of the victims or feel their pain. Instead, he read it in the reports he read, the files he created, and the information he collated.

Evans, Bhaki and Lauren all told him of the victims who passed on their thanks for bringing criminals to justice. Whenever praise came down from the brass, Evans made sure the whole team got credit.

He'd miss the satisfaction of helping to improve victim's lives, of finding the details which helped to solve cases. Most of all, he'd miss the team. Without being conceited, he knew just how much the team relied on his digital investigations.

Working both his mobile and the open line he'd kept with Bhaki, he tried to point him towards Joserand's location.

Checking Facebook again, he saw Fiona Grace had posted an update on her earlier comment.

Bastard has took off running. Can't keep up but he ran down Dalton Ave.

Paedos beware answered within seconds

On our way. We've just left the Peddy Arms.

The Pedestrian Arms was on Newtown Road, about two hundred yards from the entrance to the hospital.

Shit! I've just told him to run towards the hospital. He's running right towards them.

Turning to the wall map, he sought out the area and then posted his own comment.

Seen the dirty bastard turn left onto raffles ave. He's now running towards shadygrove rd.

While he typed, he was ringing Joserand's mobile. As expected, he got no answer.

Telling Joserand to put his phone on silent had seemed like a good idea at the time. Now it was a hindrance.

Bhaki reported he was in his car and on his way towards Dalton Avenue.

'Call me when you get there.'

Chisholm hung up and called Lauren to see where she was. As the phone rang, he used his mobile to text Joserand new instructions

Hearing Lauren had dropped Evans at the hospital, he told her of his new plan, then put in a call to Control. It was time to mobilise the troops.

*　　*　　*　　*

Joserand checked his phone and saw a missed call from Chisholm. There was also a text message warning him the gang were coming his way. The text also told him to turn right at the first opportunity.

Running at three quarter pace to conserve energy, he turned right. Within a minute, he was at Wigton Road.

Now it was decision time. Should he turn left and head for the safety of the busier central areas of the city, or should he cross the road and hide himself in suburbia? He knew there was a park surrounding a community centre, and the idea of hiding among the numerous bushes called to him. Yet he knew it was also a perfect place for an attack to go unnoticed.

Crossing Wigton Road at a sprint, he thundered along the pavement, his eyes searching for a decent hiding place. When he found one, he'd text Chisholm and let him know where he was.

*　　*　　*　　*

Chisholm kept updating the Facebook page with statuses designed to draw the vigilante group away from Joserand's position. When he'd led them into a bottleneck, he would spring his trap.

Before he dared spring the trap, he would have to locate Joserand and have him collected.

His repeated texts had gone un-answered. It didn't surprise him. If he was in Joserand's position, he wouldn't be sending texts. He'd be running for his life.

Lauren and Bhaki were circling the area looking for Joserand. Both were relying on him to pinpoint an exact location, though.

Looking at his mobile, he willed it to beep or ring, to show any kind of message or contact from Joserand.

Facebook was updated with a new status which caused him to gasp in disbelief.

Think U guys may be mistaken. Pretty sure he's just ran along Barrowvale Road.

Bloody hell. Joserand must have taken fright and crossed Wigton Road. He must be terrified.

Calling Lauren, he re-directed her towards Barrowvale Road while leaving Bhaki to watch for any sign of the gang moving in that direction.

As he spoke, he used a different profile to post to the group.

U r wrong!!! Hes jst gone by me hes running like fck so u better be quick.

The response was immediate.

Where r u?

Chisholm glanced at the map on the wall and found the perfect place to spring his trap.

By oakdale school

A flood of vitriolic comments came after his post, each poster calling Joserand worse than shit for going towards a school.

*   *   *   *

Evans ran through the hospital as fast as he could, concern for Janet powering him through the sterile atrium.

His watch told him she would be in surgery for another hour at least, but he had to be there. He had to be by her side, or as close as he could be.

Joserand and all the others could look after themselves. His place was here, with his wife, even if the here in question was a hospital waiting room. Speaking to a receptionist at the main desk, he was told to go to the Beech ward.

The receptionist had a patient manner and friendly smile, but neither was enough to lift the gloom of his spirits.

Janet had been withdrawn enough after losing the baby. Now she'd lost the chance of having another, he didn't know how he could begin to lift her spirits.

Right now, he wasn't sure he could lift his own. He felt like raging at the injustices of the world, but knew better. Theirs was a fate many couples faced and there was nothing or nobody to blame for it. Life had decided to take a kick at Mr & Mrs Harry Evans, and there was nothing to be gained from taking a kick back.

Sitting alone in the waiting room, he made repeated vows he would do whatever it took to put the smile back into Janet's eyes.

* * * *

Hiding behind a garage, Troy Joserand reached into his hoodie's front pocket. His grasping fingers could only feel the keys to his temporary home and his wallet. Checking again, he still couldn't find his mobile.

Reasoning it must have fallen out when he was running, he wracked his brains as to what he should do next.

Going back and looking for it may lead him into danger, yet doing nothing wouldn't get him to safety.

Edging his head around the garage, he scanned the street in both directions. There was no movement to be seen. No pedestrians walked the streets and the road carried no traffic.

Setting a brisk pace, he strode back the way he came, his eyes swapping between the ground and the road. A hundred yards from his hiding place, he found his mobile lying on the pavement. Snatching it up, he clutched it tight and sprinted back to the garage.

Secure in his hiding place once more, he took a proper look at the phone. Its screen was cracked and there was a nasty dent on one corner.

Shit. Please work. Please let me call that copper.

The metrics of the screen were off by a half inch, but Joserand managed to call Chisholm. He'd made a mental note of the street he was on, as Chisholm had told him to.

'DS Chisholm? It's Troy. I'm on Barrowvale Road … about halfway along. I'm behind some garages.'

Troy listened for a few seconds and then hung up.

Less than three minutes later, he heard a pair of short blasts on a car horn, followed by two longer ones.

Poking his head round the corner, he saw a red BMW M3. Approaching it with caution, he saw a pretty blonde sitting in the driver's seat. A warrant card was held out of the open window.

'You're safe. DS Chisholm led them into a trap. They're rounding up the last of them now.'

* * * *

Evans sprang to his feet as Janet was wheeled out of the lift. Her eyes found him. A single tear escaped her left eye and rolled down her cheek.

Not knowing what to say, Evans said the first thing he could think of. 'I love you so much, Janet Evans. We're gonna get through this. Together, you and I can get through anything. When you're ready, we can look at adoption or fostering.'

He took her hand in his, and held her fingers in a gentle embrace as the hospital porter pushed her bed towards the ward.

Steering her bed into a vacant space, the porter went to pass the doctor's notes to the nurse sitting behind the desk.

'Harry.' Janet's voice was a hoarse whisper, as her fingers sought out the button which controlled the morphine drip. 'I lost our baby because I was raped.'

Dealing with the Drugs

DC Lauren Phillips pulled on a black skirt and turned to examine herself in the full-length mirror on the wardrobe door. Satisfied with what she saw, she picked up her keys and a clutch bag.

Today was the first step towards getting the answers she needed. Once her questions were answered, she'd be able to inform DI Harry Evans of what she'd learned. Until she had some hard evidence, she was on her own.

The initial facts she had were sketchy at best. The one concrete lead she'd got, had come from a source too scared to testify.

Discussing it with Evans had been a disaster. Preoccupied with his wife's rape, he'd been more caustic than usual. Both her professional skills and her personal interest in the case had come under fire, leaving her smarting at his put-downs.

Determined not to let this one slip, she'd decided to pursue the case in her own time, until she could gather what was needed to prompt a formal investigation.

* * * *

Parking behind a row of cars on Peter Street, Lauren locked her car and click-clacked her way towards Finkle Street. The three hundred yard walk through the centre of Workington saw her draw stares from shoppers and people going about their everyday business.

She knew her clothing was more akin to a night on the town than four o'clock in the afternoon, but she'd dressed this way for a reason. Lauren didn't care about the disapproving looks she got from the women or the mental undressing of the men she encountered. Blessed with a pretty face and shapely body, Lauren knew she looked good, and used her charms to her advantage whenever possible.

Reaching the club, Lauren tried the door, only to find it locked. Three rounds of knocking later, it was answered by a scruffy man in his early twenties. Lauren waited for the obligatory scan of her figure.

When Scruffy was finished examining her body, he took a moment to look at Lauren's face. 'You here for the interview?'

'That's right. I'm Monique.' Lauren held out a hand, hoping Scruffy was the one who'd interview her. The way he'd looked at her, she was sure he'd give her the job.

'Mr Nicholson is through here.'

Scruffy turned on his heel and led her into the club. Looking around, Lauren saw pretty much what she'd expected to see. A long bar filled one wall, while the opposite side was lined with leather bench seats arranged in a series of crescents. At the far end of the narrow room were a series of booths with red velour curtains hanging from brass rails.

'Grab a seat. I'll get Mr Nicholson.' Scruffy took off towards a door marked 'Private', behind the bar.

The centre of the room was dominated by two poles, set on waist-high platforms. Each of the walls had burgundy flocked wallpaper and pictures of models posing in their underwear.

The smell of stale beer and unspent testosterone hung in the air. The lighting was muted, although there were a series of unlit spotlights pointing at the twin stages.

Lauren supposed she ought to feel nervous applying for a job as a lap-dancer, but she didn't feel even the slightest twinge of apprehension. An exhibitionist by nature, she enjoyed the attention her body got her and she took a care to always make the most of her assets.

The higher purpose which brought her here eradicated any fears she may have about exposing her body to a bunch of strangers. The biggest worries for Lauren were failing to get the evidence she needed or her superiors finding out and firing her.

Either would spell disaster and mean Peter Nicholson getting off scot free. She'd researched Nicholson on the Police National Database and had found him to be a smooth, if shady, operator. Linked to many petty criminals, he'd managed to amass a share of Cumbria's organised crime without stepping on the toes of the Leighton family, with enough weight to start a turf war. Arrested numerous times, he'd never been charged thanks to a rapacious lawyer who always found a way to nullify investigations.

Lauren recognised the man following Scruffy as Peter Nicholson. Well groomed, the black hair above his handsome face had the first showings of silvery grey.

Rising to her feet, Lauren extended a hand. 'Hi, I'm Monique.'

Nicholson took the hand and smiled, his appraisal of her far quicker than Scruffy's.

'Peter Nicholson.' He took a seat and gestured for her to do the same. When she was seated, he turned to Scruffy. 'You can go now. I'll take it from here.'

Scruffy managed to look disappointed while scowling at his boss's back. As he disappeared through the door behind the bar, Nicholson picked up the clipboard he'd carried with him.

'I've a few questions for you and then I'd like you to demonstrate your dancing skills. Are you okay with that?'

'Sure.' Lauren nodded and hoped he didn't see how false her smile was.

'First off, have you worked as a dancer before?'

'No.'

Nicholson's eyebrows lifted a half inch. 'Do you know what's expected of dancers in a place like this?'

'Of course. Men will pay me to strip for them.' Lauren didn't mention she'd researched lap dancing on the internet and had been to the lap dancing club in Carlisle, where she'd had a couple of dances to supplement what she'd learned online.

'And you're okay with that?'

'That depends on how much they expect for their money.'

It was Nicholson's turn to nod. 'The rates in here are ten pounds for topless and twenty for nude.'

'What would I get from that?' Lauren cursed herself. She hadn't wanted to come across as too intelligent, and here she was, turning the interview around and setting the questions.

'You get the full amount. We charge a dancing fee of seventy-five pounds per night. Anything the dancers make over and above that is their own business.'

'Okaaay.' Lauren stretched the word as if considering his proposal. She didn't care about the money. Financial gain wasn't the reason she was applying for this job.

'Technically, you won't be working for me. You'll be self-employed, and therefore you'll be responsible for paying your own taxes.'

'Fair enough.'

'Make no mistake, though.' A steely look touched Nicholson's eyes. 'I'm the one in charge and the dancers all answer to me.'

'Of course.'

'So why are you applying for a job here? You're smarter than the usual girls who apply.'

Lauren hesitated, as if reluctant to answer. 'I've got credit card debt I need to get rid of. When that's cleared, I want to start saving for a house. I've been in debt too long and I'm not having it anymore.'

Her answer was designed to show commitment to the job, to show she was in it for the long haul and wouldn't be leaving after a couple of weeks.

'Sounds familiar.' A wry smile touched Nicholson's lips. 'Now, getting to the meat of the sandwich, do you think you're going to be able to strip knowing men are staring at you?'

Lauren stood up and gestured at her clothes. 'I've just walked through the middle of Workington dressed like this. How much of a problem do you think I have with people looking at me?'

Nicholson's eyes scanned her body from top to toe for a second time. She felt his eyes as they slid down the lacy top she wore and onto the miniskirt.

Turning around, she let him see the transparent back of her top that showed she wasn't wearing a bra. Lifting the hem of her skirt, she gave him a glimpse of her stocking tops.

'So you're not shy, then.' Nicholson smiled as he spoke. 'I want to see you dance. I need to know that you've got the moves and that you're not all talk.'

'Fair enough.' Lauren had expected no less. Nobody in their right minds would employ a stripper without seeing them strip.

Nicholson walked over to the bar and fiddled with a music system. As he returned, a dance tune filled the otherwise silent club.

Lauren waited until he was seated and then, mimicking the dancer she'd hired in Carlisle, she rested his hands on his knees. Gyrating in time with the beat, she began a slow and sensual lap dance.

Nicholson watched her with a cold detachment that would have un-nerved her had she not felt the bulge of his erection. One by one, she went through the moves she'd learned from her experience in Carlisle.

When the track ended, she was naked apart from stockings and suspenders. Taking a seat opposite Nicholson, she put her clothes beside her and looked him in the eye.

'So, have I got the job?'

'Yes. You can start tonight. We open at nine.' His eyes narrowed. 'Are you sure you've never done this before?'

Lauren reached for her thong. 'Not for money.'

* * * *

Harry Evans laid down his book and looked across at his wife. She was holding a book of her own, but he could see from her glazed expression that she wasn't reading it.

Since telling him of her rape, she had become a different person. The thousand-watt smile had dimmed and while she pretended to put on a brave face, he could see she was distracted by dark thoughts.

He knew the dangers of dark thoughts, how they possessed the mind, influencing every decision, every word spoken and the tone it was delivered in.

His own dark thoughts had sent him to the brink of oblivion before he mustered enough self-control to haul himself back. It wasn't for himself he returned. It was for Janet. He knew she needed him more than he'd ever been needed before.

He'd reported the rape, as was his duty. Yet he'd tried to find the rapist himself, so he could enact a different kind of justice. A biblical justice delivered with an un-lubricated baseball bat. A medieval justice.

His colleagues in the police had kept him away from the investigation, held him back when he'd tried to attack Derek Yates in his cell.

He knew they'd done the right thing, but he'd happily give everything he owned for two minutes alone with the man who'd raped his wife.

His and Janet's lives would never be the same thanks to Yates' actions. They'd be forever tarnished by loss. Stained by memories and thoughts of what might have been.

Reaching across the couch, he took Janet's hand in his. 'They've got him. He's going down for life and will never see the light of day again.'

Janet said nothing. Her face didn't even register she'd heard his words.

He squeezed her fingers just hard enough to get her attention. 'I'm off shift at six tomorrow. I'll take you to that place you like at Keswick for a bite to eat if you like.'

When Janet spoke, her voice was flat and lifeless, her attempts at normality failing. 'I can't. I said I'd cover for Jessica, so I'll be there until midnight. Maybe next week, eh?'

'Whenever you want.' Evans planted a tender kiss on her knuckles and lifted his book.

Try as he might, he couldn't get the words on the page to focus. His eyes were forever travelling further afield, searching for a past happiness no longer visible.

He knew his team were behind him and he appreciated the way they were absorbing his bad temper and ignoring his abusive comments. He couldn't tell them as much, but he'd take them for a drink or spring for the fast food the next time they had to work late. Chisholm would understand his intentions and explain them to Bhaki and Lauren if they didn't work it out for themselves.

*   *   *   *

Lauren entered Shakers and looked around, seeking either Nicholson or Scruffy. Finding Scruffy at the far end of the room exchanging angry words with an emaciated girl, Lauren approached in such a way that she neither interrupted them nor remained unseen.

As she got closer, Lauren could see the girl sported recent bruising around her left eye. Makeup had been used to disguise any discolouring, but it couldn't hide the swelling or the burst blood vessels in the corner of her eye.

Scruffy turned his head and flicked his eyes at Lauren. A nod of recognition was followed by a raised finger.

Turning back to the unfortunate girl, Scruffy jabbed a finger towards her face. 'Piss off home and don't come back until you're fit to work.'

Every instinct Lauren possessed as a police officer screamed at her to find out how the girl had got a black eye, but she knew it would unmask her to Scruffy. Burying the urge to inquire, she gave a tight smile instead. 'Is there anything I need to know before I start?'

Scruffy looked her up and down, his eyes resting on her breasts for an uncomfortable length of time. When his assessment was complete, a finger pointed to the back of the room.

'The booths are over there, the customers come in the front door, and there's a small changing room at the back where you can keep your stuff.'

'Got it.'

'If a customer tries to grab you, you push his hand away. If he tries again, yell for help. One of the bouncers will deal with him.'

'Fair enough.' Lauren wasn't worried about defending herself against wandering hands. Looking and dressing the way she did, she was accustomed to having her bum pinched or the feel of a sweaty hand attempting to take liberties.

'As far as your own conduct is concerned, if we hear of you making propositions or of you sleeping with the customers after your shift then you're out on your arse.'

'What do you take me for? I'm doing this to get myself out of a financial hole not to catch God knows what.' Lauren filled her voice with indignant outrage, but she'd expected the warning. Strip clubs were always associated with brothels and she wanted to lay down her marker before Scruffy or Nicholson miscounted two and two.

Her indignance would also serve to keep them from getting any ideas about her availability.

Scruffy gave a lackadaisical shrug. 'You wouldn't be the first to try it, and I don't expect you'd be the last.'

Three girls walked in together. Dressed in jeans and jackets, their bored expressions didn't inspire Lauren with confidence.

Scruffy waved them over and pointed at Lauren. 'This is Monique. She's starting tonight, so show her the ropes.'

Looking at the trio, Lauren felt the first stirrings of animosity. A tall blonde with an acne-scarred face held out a limp hand

'Katya.' Her thumb jerked to her left then right as she made the other introductions. 'This is Scarlett and Candy. We get changed and then talk proper.'

The way Katya spoke, the promised talk was inferred as more of a threat than a helpful showing of the ropes.

Despite herself, Lauren began to feel the first prickles of apprehension. Now she was here and about to embark on a stripping career, the unfamiliar feeling of butterflies in her stomach threatened to have her sprinting for the bathroom.

Steeling her nerves, Lauren walked around the room, getting an in-depth feel for it. As she went, she made mental notes of the dark corners, the angles which would see lights flashing into eyes and the areas best covered by the CCTV cameras.

Looking at the clock on the wall, she saw it was almost nine and there still wasn't any sign of the girls emerging from the cramped changing room. They either mustn't care about not being ready for when the doors opened, or they knew from experience they didn't have to be ready as it would be quiet at first.

Regardless of the reason for their tardiness, Lauren wanted to try and befriend them. The key to her getting the information she needed lay in how well she was liked and trusted by the staff and management of Shakers.

Candy was the first to appear. Her dumpy body was clad in a loose fitting babydoll which did little to hide the rolls of flab sagging over the top of her lace knickers.

Lauren greeted her with a smile, only for Candy to ignore her and head for the bar, where she handed Scruffy a sheaf of notes.

Realising she too would have to pay her way, Lauren joined her at the bar and reached into her purse.

'D'you think it'll get busy later?'

Candy didn't look at her, but at least she answered. 'I bloody hope so. I need every penny I can get.'

'I know what you mean.' Lauren tried a conspiratorial smile. 'I'm only here for the money too.'

'So pretty new girl is here for the money too. She make sure all girls get fair number of dances, she be allowed to stay.'

Lauren whirled round to find Katya right behind her, a malevolent look on her face. Scarlett was at Katya's side, her bikini-clad body showcasing a tapestry of eclectic tattoos set against pale flesh.

'What do you mean allowed to stay? I'm just here to make as much money as possible so I can pay off my debts. Surely it's Mr Nicholson's decision about who works here, not yours.'

Lauren couldn't stop herself from snapping the angry reply at Katya. Too often, she had seen first-hand the damage caused by bullies and their aggressive ways. She'd learned the best way to deal with such behaviour was to challenge it from the start and then let the chips fall where they may. Yet she didn't want to pick a fight with any of the girls working here. Not when she needed them to confide in her, to trust her with their secrets.

Katya's false nail jabbed into Lauren's chest. 'You not have to be fired to stop working here. You maybe decide quit. Yes?'

'No.' Lauren held Katya's eye. 'I'm here because I need the money. If you can't handle a little bit of competition, maybe it's you who should quit.'

'Pah! You no dancer. You last five minutes. You no competition for me.'

'Then what's your problem?'

Katya didn't answer her. Instead, she went behind the bar and whispered into Scruffy's ear. Lauren couldn't tell what was said, but she didn't like the way a broad smirk painted itself on Scruffy's face.

Before she could begin to guess, a group of men came into the bar. From their dirty clothes and hob-nailed boots, she figured they were involved in the building of the new supermarket on the outskirts of town.

Although clearly under the effects of the alcohol they'd drank since finishing time, they weren't too rowdy. A spotty-faced youth in the middle of the group was the only one who appeared to be drunk.

The lad's eyes oscillated around the room until they settled on Lauren. An unsubtle elbow was dug into the ribs of the man at his side as a wobbling arm was pointed in her direction.

Unsure whether to approach the lad or let him come to her, Lauren's momentary hesitation gave the more experienced Katya the opportunity she needed.

Lauren could do nothing except watch as Katya sashayed her way towards the lad, her intentions to steal his custom quite blatant. Her thin body, clad only in a bra and thong, attracted his gaze when she got close enough for his bleary eyes to focus on her obvious charms.

Scarlet and Candy followed her lead and set off towards the men, their attempts at alluring sexiness forced and unnatural.

Understanding the protocol, Lauren caught the eye of a forty-something man who appeared to be the natural leader of the group and made her way towards him.

Each step taken forward caused the growing knot of tension to tighten in her stomach. Unfamiliar with the sensation, Lauren had to battle the flight instinct screaming at her to run for the door.

The overriding feeling swirling through her brain was that she was out of her depth. It was one thing to wear clothes which gave discreet flashes, it was quite another to seduce men into paying for her to strip. It was only the thought of Christopher lying in the hospital bed which kept her to her intended purpose.

'Hi. I'm Monique.'

'Tom.' The builder smiled at her and kept his eyes on her face. 'Been busy?'

Lauren shook her head, smiling at the banality of the conversation. 'Not yet. We've only just opened for the night.'

Tom nodded, his eyes stealing a glance at her lace covered chest. 'Oh, right'-

Whatever he was about to say was drowned out by Scruffy's voice on the microphone.

'Ladies and gentlemen, would you please put your hands together for the beautiful, the flexible, the desirable, Candy.' His words were met with a fierce scowl from Candy and a resigned look from the other two girls, as a few polite handclaps echoed over the music.

Candy left the group of men she was with and made her way to the nearest of the two stages. As she climbed the three steep steps, the music dipped as Scruffy made another announcement.

'Coming later tonight, we have a special Shakers event. A dance-off between two of our loveliest dancers. The sultry Monique has challenged our reigning champion Mistress Katya to a fully nude dance off. The loser will buy everyone in the bar a beer. Tell your friends and get them here. It's gonna be epiiic.'

Lauren tried to process this information as Scruffy held the last syllable in the style of a boxing commentator. Glancing around, she saw Katya give her a confident wink.

That bitch has set me up.

The anger coursing through her veins loosened the knot in her stomach and filled her with an extra determination. Not only would she stick this out to get justice for Christopher, she'd damn well make sure she beat Katya in the dance-off.

'You didn't know about that, did you?'

'No, I didn't.' Lauren was honest with Tom, but annoyed at herself for letting her surprise show.

Her next words took a lot out of her, but she had a role to play and knew what she must do to play the part.

'No thanks. I'm only here because of that lot.' A thumb indicated Tom's workmates.

'No problem.' Lauren wondered at the etiquette of leaving, now she knew Tom wasn't going to pay for a dance. Figuring on an exit strategy, she flashed him a genuine smile. 'Let me know if you change your mind.'

His hand landed on her wrist, his fingers coarse with calluses, but his touch gentle. 'Stay and talk for a minute. So long as she's up there, this lot won't be interested in anything else.'

Lauren recognised the truth in Tom's words. While Candy was giving a free show, nobody would be interested in paying for a private dance.

As she chatted with Tom, she kept her eyes on what was happening elsewhere in the room. Katya was stood in the middle of the group, with a proprietal arm draped around the drunk lad.

On stage, Candy twirled and posed in a series of faux seductive moves. As the song neared its end, Candy's fingers found the clasp at the front of the babydoll she wore. Undoing the clasp, she teased the material to either side with a deliberate slowness, until her breasts were exposed. A faint cheer went up from one or two of the builders, although the majority just looked for a moment and then turned their attention back to the drinks in their hands.

Lauren felt embarrassed for Candy. A group of half-pissed builders hadn't been impressed by the sight of her flaccid breasts dangling over her lumpen stomach. While she'd not expected any glory in this role, she knew a kick in the teeth when she saw one.

The response of the builders retied the knot in her stomach as doubts began to assail her.

What if they turn away from me like that? What if I get even worse from them?

A voice at her ear and a hand on her elbow interrupted her doubts.

'Scuse me. Can you give me a dansch?'

It was the drunk lad. Behind him stood a glowering Katya.

'Sure.'

The single word had been spoken before Lauren had time to consider its implications. Everything she'd done up until now could be explained away if her superiors found out. Now she'd agreed to accept money for stripping, there was no going back. The line had been crossed.

'D'you want a ten or twenty pound dance?' Again the words came without thought, making Lauren realise just how much she'd unconsciously immersed herself into the undercover role. She almost felt as if she was watching herself in some kind of weird out-of-body experience.

'Twenty please.'

'C'mon, then.'

Lauren led the youth towards the booths at the back of the room, as new doubts assailed her.

Christ! He doesn't look old enough to drink. Am I about to expose myself to a minor?

A self-preserving sense of reason kicked in and offered some reassurance to counteract the doubts.

Don't be soft. He wouldn't have been able to get drunk if he was seriously underage. Besides, I'm protected by the door policy. It's their job to make sure the people in here are at least twenty-one.

It could have been a lot worse. This lad's eyes are so glassy, he'll hardly see me.

Lauren pulled back the curtain and ushered the lad into the three-by-six foot booth. Taking the twenty pounds from his hand, she positioned him on the stool and started to move in time with the music.

As she danced, Lauren kept her eyes on his, alert for any sign of boredom or the intent to reach out. Beer fumes rose from the lad as she gyrated her way to nudity.

Watching his eyes lock onto her bare breasts and then her more intimate areas, Lauren felt a transfer of power in the poorly-lit booth. She'd entered the booth at his request, lured by the money in his pocket. Just another purchase made after a few beers on payday.

Yet the unrestrained lust in his eyes put him in her control. It was her who called the shots and he who said thank you first.

Lauren was used to using her body to get whatever she wanted, but dancing for this lad had shown her a whole new level of control was available. He'd fallen under her spell long before any clothing had been removed, and the experience of dancing for him dispelled all her nerves and self-doubts.

Letting the lad exit the booth first, Lauren put her clothes back on and emerged to see a few more men had come in. Scarlett and Katya were nowhere to be seen, but Candy was trying her luck with the new faces.

The young lad's voice carried across the room as he was teased by his older colleagues. 'Fucking brilliant. You should try her.'

* * * *

Time passed quickly for Lauren as more and more new faces piled into the club. By observing the other dancers, she soon learned the men to target and the best way to get them to part with their money. Her purse bulged with notes taken from beer-filled men intent on getting a cheap thrill.

Some of the men seemed to be regulars, as they commented on not having seen her before. Others appeared to be here for the first time, their behaviour nervous, as if they were unsure of how to conduct themselves.

Frequent reminders from Scruffy had built up expectation for the dance-off. Unsure when it would be, Lauren wasn't able to inform the men who asked her. Whenever she tried pressing Scruffy, he just said 'later'.

Looking around, she saw the young lad coming her way once more. She'd already danced for him three times, but he seemed to be coming back for a forth turn. He was now so drunk he was slurring to the point of incomprehension, his eyes almost blank and unseeing.

Lauren felt guilty taking his money, aware that tomorrow morning would bring him nothing but a raging hangover and an empty pocket. If he was lucky, he might be able to remember the first time she'd danced.

When the dance ended, Lauren exited the booth to see a face which filled her with dread.

Walking towards the booths behind Katya was a face from her past. Ten years ago, Mr Simmons had been her geography teacher. Bored by his turgid style of teaching, she had spent most of his lessons giggling with friends.

Even at a young age, she'd been aware of his attentions. Understanding he fancied her and some of her mates, she pushed the boundaries of acceptable classroom behaviour secure in the knowledge that he wouldn't administer any of his threatened punishments. The same behaviour in other classrooms would have seen her marched to the headmaster's office, but "Creepy Simmons" was a pushover for a pretty face.

She looked at the floor as she passed him, more afraid that being recognised would fuel his fantasies than of being exposed. The lecherous fool would get immense kicks from the knowledge and, while she could refuse to dance for him, it would raise suspicions. Besides, in light of the dance-off, there was going to be no hiding from him.

I hope he buggers off before then.

Scruffy's voice cut across the air with a booming excitement. 'Ladies and gentlemen, I have just been informed that tonight's dance-off between the sultry Monique and Mistress Katya will take place in just five minutes. Fill your glasses and get ready to fill your boots. It's gonna be awwwwesome.'

'Have you time for a quick dance?'

The speaker was one of the builders. Figuring they couldn't start without her, Lauren nodded. 'Would you like a ten or twenty pound dance?'

'How about a superior dance?'

'Sorry. I don't know what you mean.' The builder's face changed in an instant. 'Erm, a tenner.'

As Lauren danced for the builder, she felt a stab of exultant vindication. She'd been waiting all night for someone to ask for a deluxe, superior or executive dance.

The three words each represented a different kind of order. Her cousin Christopher had learned of this ordering system when visiting Shakers on a night out with friends. Unknown to him, the ecstasy tablet which came with his deluxe dance was from a dangerous batch.

Within an hour of taking the tablet, he'd suffered a neurological collapse on the right side of his brain. He now lay in a hospital bed in an induced coma, while doctors waited to see if his brain could repair itself from the damage wrought by the toxins.

Since hearing the news, Lauren had bullied, demanded and coaxed information from those in his company on that fateful night. They'd told her how Christopher was fine one minute and on the ground fitting the next.

Now she'd been asked for a superior dance, she knew she was on the right track, all doubts about being here assuaged by confirmation of the stories she'd been told. Knowing for certain didn't make it any less risky, to either her health or career if she was uncovered, but it did give her the confidence to see it through.

Returning to the club floor after the dance, Lauren saw Scruffy waving her across to where he and Katya stood at the bar.

Now she had confirmation, it was all Lauren could do not to claw Katya's eyes out. Tempting as the thought was, Lauren knew a greater satisfaction was to be had from bringing down Nicholson and whoever was behind the supply routes.

Scruffy looked at each of them in turn. 'You's ready?'

Not bothering to listen to their answers, he climbed onto the bar and raised the microphone to his lips.

'Iiiiit's here! That's right, ladies and gentlemen, the time you've all been waiting for has arrived. We're about to start a Shakers dance-off between the sultry Monique and the devilishly dirty Mistress Katya. The girls will dance to two tracks each and you can decide on your favourite. The loser will buy every one of you a beer, while the winner will be crowned Shakers' champion.'

A host of cheers rang around the bar, but now the moment was at hand, Lauren's nerves had evaporated. Armed with the surety of conviction, she felt invincible. She would beat Katya.

She would gain the approval of Scruffy and Nicholson. The approach to deliver the more exotic dances would soon be made, and then she'd have her evidence.

She wasn't sure how she was going to explain having the evidence, but that was a bridge she'd cross when she came to it.

'First up, we have the lovely, the bow-dacious. Miiistress Katya.'

Katya made her way onto one of the podiums, playing up to the crowd as she went. As the music began, she embraced the pole and effortlessly hauled herself towards the ceiling. Halfway up the pole, she stopped climbing and sat in an upright position, held in place by the strength of her thighs.

Unhooking her bra she let herself fall backwards, flinging her arms towards the podium, the move leaving her topless and upside down. Retaking the pole in her hands, she somersaulted backwards and went straight into a series of gyrations.

Lauren watched with an analytical eye. Katya had the moves and was brazen enough to follow through on them, but there was no grace or style about her or her act. Once exposed from the bra, her implanted breasts sat immobile on her chest like half grapefruits, her moves were more look-at-what-I'm-prepared-to-do than seduction or enticement.

Katya was naked for the whole of the second song, and she used the time to display her prowess with the pole while making sure every man in the room got an eyeful.

Scruffy led the round of applause and the cheering, before introducing Lauren to the baying crowd.

Taking her place on the other podium, Lauren was grateful Katya had warmed the crowd up first.

She took a different approach to Katya and went for subtle seduction rather than shock and awe, only starting to remove her clothes when the second song kicked in. When the last item of her clothing hit the floor, it was greeted with a loud cheer.

As the music faded out, Scruffy stood on the bar and called for order. When the crowd had quietened down, he raised the microphone to his lips.

'Gentlemen, I have Mistress Katya on my right and Monique on my left. Please cast your vote by moving towards whichever girl gets your vote.'

It took a couple of minutes, but soon all the men in the room had cast their vote.

Lauren's podium was surrounded by two-thirds of the men in the room, making her the clear winner. Katya face twisted into a vicious scowl when Scruffy announced the result, despite nobody needing to hear the official verdict.

Lauren received several requests for a private dance and, by the time she'd worked her way through those prepared to wait their turn, Scruffy and the barman had served all the beers Katya had to stand.

Scarlett and Candy were kept busy with dances, but Katya was getting nowhere. Every time she approached someone, they shook their head. Had she not hated Katya with every fibre of her body, she would have pitied the woman.

Once the free beers were consumed, the place started to empty out.

Having decided to take the bull by the horns, Lauren approached Scruffy. 'I was asked for a superior dance earlier. What are those?'

His eyes flickered left, indicating he was using the right side of his brain. The creative side. A lie was on its way. 'I dunno. Maybe it's what the girls call a two girl experience. Ask the girls. They'll tell you.'

Lauren thanked him and turned away. She needed time to think about the best way to approach the girls.

Candy seemed to be the friendliest, but both she and Scarlett obeyed Katya's every command. To get the answers she needed, she'd have to engineer some time alone with Candy.

*   *   *   *

Harry Evans stamped through the corridors of Durranhill Station. Janet had endured another restless night interspersed with nightmares and uncontrollable sobbing fits. When he'd left their flat, she had only just fallen into a dreamless slumber.

Finding Lauren absent, he demanded Chisholm tell him where she was.

'She's on her way, guv. I reckon she'll be here in five minutes.' Chisholm followed his words with a pointed look at his watch. Their shift wasn't due to start for another fifteen minutes.

'She'd better be here soon.'

Chisholm kept quiet and refocused his gaze on the twin computer screens on his desk, while Evans scowled at the piece of paper clutched in his hand.

'What the fuck is this supposed to mean? I mean, what the fuck do Mungo and Martins think they are playing at? This report is so full of shite, it should have been sent to a sewage farm.'

'Morning all. Is there a problem, guv?' Lauren greeted them with a smile, and passed around the containers of coffee she brought in every morning.

'Aye, there's a fucking problem. I should've been a proctologist, the number of arseholes I have to deal with.'

'The M&Ms?' Lauren directed her question to Chisholm, who nodded in confirmation.

'Never mind that just now.' Evans pointed at the door. 'Shut that and then sit down.'

Lauren took her usual seat, and then looked at Evans with innocent enquiry all over her face.

'What's up?'

'What did you learn at Shakers last night?'

'I beg your pardon?'

'Don't even try and deny it. I had Jabba trace your mobile yesterday. You went to Shakers for an hour in the late afternoon then you were there from nine until just after one.' Evans took a sip of his coffee. 'When you came to me with those allegations, I could tell you weren't going to take no for an answer. I know what you're like. There's no way you'd let it go, after what happened to your cousin. The next logical step for you was to get a job there and try to get enough evidence to convince me to look into it.'

Lauren's face flushed with anger as she rose to her feet and leaned across the desk at Evans.

'I thought you'd try to stop me if I told you what I planned to do. Instead, you worked it out and let me do it anyway. I don't like being used. I don't like it one little bit.'

'And I don't like members of my team going behind my back, taking unauthorised undercover roles. Especially when they're stripping.'

'Then why didn't you stop me?'

'Would you have listened if I tried to talk you out of it?' Evans waved a hand. 'Don't even bother to answer. We all know you wouldn't. The only way to stop you was to grass you up to the brass or to Nicholson. You'd have lost your career or Nicholson would have cleaned up his act. Yes, I have been using you. I'll admit that. But what you don't know is that I had Jabba watching the front of the club and Bhaki watching the back. If you'd left through either door with anyone, they'd have called backup and then stepped in.'

Lauren's jaw hung open for a second before she recovered her composure. 'So you posted lookouts? What do you think would have happened if they'd been spotted?'

Evans gave a non-committal shrug.

'I'll tell you what would have bloody happened. My cover would have been blown and then I'd never be able to prove where Christopher got that dodgy ecstasy tablet from.' Lauren fixed Evans with a ferocious stare. 'Either back me or sack me. But don't ever use me.'

Evans looked down at his desk. 'I was backing you, Lauren. You were off the books investigating a lead which we didn't have enough proof to follow. What would you have had me do? Send in a gang of plain clothes coppers from another area? They'd have been rumbled in minutes. The only way to handle this was to let you do your own thing and provide discreet support.'

Lauren slumped back into her seat.

'Here.' Chisholm extended his hand towards Lauren. A small jewellery case was between his fingers. 'Gi'e's your mobile.'

'Why?' The fight had evaporated from her as she realised Evans' hands had been tied by bureaucracy and her actions.

'I'm gonna put an app onto it which'll let me listen to anything the microphones in these earrings pickup.'

Lauren's eyes narrowed. 'I've never heard of anything like this in the police tech armoury. Where'd you get it from?'

Chisholm pointed at his computer. 'Courtesy of a certain Mr Google and the guv's credit card.'

*   *   *   *

Lauren walked into Shakers with a confident strut. Now she had the backing of Harry Evans and the rest of the team, she felt the odds of getting a result had taken a big swing in her favour.

Her shift last Saturday had passed without event. Katya had left her alone and nobody had asked her for anything other than an ordinary dance.

She had her suspicions, though. Candy seemed to get more than her fair share of dances. Which, considering her looks, rang alarm bells. Coupled with the high number of people who came in, had one dance with her, then left, it seemed obvious she was the main supplier.

Lauren had also noticed the men who took a dance with Candy often spoke to Katya first.

She didn't need her detective skills to work out Katya was in charge of the operation and was referring the men onto Candy.

Dropping her bag into the changing room, she interrupted a hissed exchange between Katya and Scarlett. Candy was nowhere to be seen. Whatever they were arguing about, it was clear Scarlett was saying no to Katya.

Scarlett stormed out. Lauren pretended she hadn't noticed their argument, and began to change into the outfit she'd chosen for tonight's shift.

'I want talk to you.'

'What is it?' Lauren looked at Katya, expecting another bout of antagonism.

'We get off on … how you say? Wrong leg?'

Lauren didn't correct her, didn't trust herself to speak. Whatever Katya was up to, it seemed an olive branch was about to be offered. Inside her chest, her heart thumped hard metronomic beats as adrenaline coursed through her system.

'True.'

'I be bitch for no reason. Am sorry.'

'Fair enough.'

Lauren bent down and picked up one of her shoes, desperate to appear cool, even though she could feel the prickles of excited sweat starting to form on her body. Balancing on one leg, she wriggled the shoe onto her foot, waiting for Katya to continue while trying to appear indifferent.

'You good dancer. Men like you, want lots of dances.'

Lauren threw out a baited hook. 'Shame they don't want more dances. I need every penny I can get.'

'Do you want make extra money?' Katya gave the smile of a predator looking at wounded prey.

'Depends what I have to do to make it. I ain't doing porn or sleeping with anyone.'

'Is not porn.' Katya straightened her back, indignance written all over her face. 'I not prostitute.'

'Sorry.'

Lauren tried to put contrition on her face as she thought of a way to get the conversation back on track. It wasn't her intention to halt Katya's flow, but she knew she had to stay in the role she'd assumed.

Katya rescued her. 'Way to make money is easier.'

'What is it, then? What would I have to do?'

'When men ask for deluxe, superior or executive dance you give ten pound dance and special packet. Take fifty pounds off men. You keep ten for dance and get extra ten for delivering packages. Rest goes to Kevin at end of night.'

Lauren could feel the power of Katya's gaze as she pretended to consider the proposal. This was exactly what she wanted and, by mentioning Kevin, Katya also implicated Scruffy and by extension Nicholson.

She just hoped Chisholm's gadget had recorded the conversation. It had worked fine when they'd tested it, but too often, technology failed at the critical moment.

Remembering the discussions with Evans and the rest of the team, she knew she would have to play things very cleverly. The recording they were getting wouldn't stand up in court, and all the evidence they had so far would expose Lauren's undercover role. What they needed to do was catch Kevin or Katya with the drugs on them, and press them for a confession. If either could be turned, they would be able to bring down Nicholson or, at the very least, force the closure of this club.

'I'll do it.' Lauren looked Katya in the eye. 'I'm guessing I shouldn't ask what's in the packages, should I?'

'Up to you.' Katya reached into her bag and pulled out a brown paper bag. 'Is five of each in here. All marked.'

Lauren peeked into the bag and saw a collection of paper wraps. Each was marked with a letter identifying the dance it belonged to.

Leaning close to Katya, Lauren whispered in her ear. 'Which one is the charlie, and do I get a discount?'

Katya's smile was rapacious as she digested Lauren's question.

'Is marked with S. No discount, but is good stuff. Worth every penny.'

Lauren stashed the content of the paper bag in her purse and walked into the main room. She had to fight to keep the smile off her face. If Chisholm had heard the conversation with Katya, he would be beginning to mobilise the troops.

The plan was that she was to pretend to sell out of the drugs and ask for more. Once she'd done that, she was to go outside for a cigarette. Once outside, she would be seen by Chisholm, who would issue the order to go. She'd have a minute to get to the bar along the street and lose herself in the crowd so she wasn't picked up by the local plod when they raided the club.

If anything went wrong or there was a need for her to leave, Amir Bhaki would walk into the club.

Working throughout the evening, Lauren was only asked for a special dance once. Complimenting the man on his shirt, she did her best to describe him so he could be allowed to slip through the net, lest his arrest led to her exposure.

Lauren caught Katya's attention, after completing several dances. A moment later, she saw Katya excuse herself from the man she'd been trying to entice into a dance.

'Yes?'

'I need some more S. I've none left and only two E.'

Katya's eyes sparkled. 'I speak Kevin. Get more for you. You got money?'

Lauren took Katya into the nearest booth and handed over a sheaf of notes. 'I'm going out for a quick smoke. I'll get them when I come back in.'

Pulling a pack of cigarettes from her purse, Lauren made her way to the door. As she walked through the room, she saw Katya making her way to the bar.

Stepping into the street, Lauren gave a shiver as the night air enshrouded her exposed skin. She'd chosen to wear a skimpy dress which would be alluring to the customers of Shakers, yet still decent enough to be worn on a night out in a town like Workington.

As she strode along the street as fast as her heels would allow, Lauren drew on a cigarette while calling Chisholm for an update.

Hearing his voice, she went straight into her report without any salutations. 'I'm out and clear and on my way to the Blue Bell now.'

Lauren pressed the phone against her ear as a souped-up Clio trundled by, a thumping bass accompanying its movement like thudding footsteps.

'What's that? ... Cool.'

Flicking her cigarette butt down a drain, she popped a mint into her mouth and slunk into the Blue Bell. Making her way to the ladies, she found a vacant cubicle and whipped her dress over her head and turned it inside out. The reversible dress was transformed from fire-engine red to coal black.

Leaving the cubicle, she washed the thick makeup from her face and tied her long hair into a pony tail. With her transformation complete, Lauren made her way back into the crowded bar.

Picking up an empty wine glass from a table, Lauren made her way to the bar and stepped into a space vacated by a large woman with distressed hair and too many ear piercings. 'Can I get another Pinot Grigio please, gorgeous?'

The barman who served her was all smiles and she flirted with him as he served her. Using all her charm, she reeled him in until he was asking for her number. She gave a false one along with a fictional name.

With her alibi established, Lauren stepped to the back of the room and waited for her phone to ring. The plan was that she'd wait in the Blue Bell until the raid was in progress, then slip out of a back door where Amir Bhaki would be waiting to pick her up. Chisholm had checked in advance, and the back entrance of the Blue Bell wasn't covered by any CCTV cameras.

It was essential to the whole investigation that Lauren wasn't identified as the source of the tip-off they were acting upon. They'd even covered her tracks to the extent that the mobile she was using tonight was a throwaway one, her own left at home so it couldn't identify her presence at the club.

Slipping out the back door as arranged, Lauren climbed into Bhaki's car and looked at him.

Seeing the grave expression on his face, Lauren felt her stomach drop. 'What's wrong? Has the raid not gone ahead?'

'Yeah. They're in there now. I watched them go in. They'll get them.'

'So, what's wrong?'

Bhaki didn't answer until he was stopped by the traffic lights at the corner of Washington Street.

'It's the guv's wife.'

Lauren's stomach sank another foot. Whatever Bhaki was about to say wouldn't be good news.

'He found her a couple of hours ago. He tried to resuscitate her, but couldn't. The paramedics couldn't either.'

'No!'

The one word couldn't begin to express the anguish Lauren felt for Evans. He'd tried to be stoic throughout recent events, but she knew how much it was affecting him. She'd seen the effort it took him to continue working, to hold it together in the face of criminals trying to get under his skin.

Questions started to present themselves. Unanswerable questions, arriving unbidden. There was just one question that mattered to her right now.

'How's the guv?'

Bhaki shook his head. 'I don't know. Chisholm tried calling him, but he's not answering. We only found out when Jenny from Control told Chisholm.'

Another question pressed at her mind. One she should probably have asked first. As she asked it, she recognised it for the straw-grasping it was. 'How did it happen? Was she attacked again?'

Once more, Bhaki's head shook. 'There's no details yet, but there's no word of suspicious circumstances.'

Washed Up

DC Amir Bhaki parked in a gateway and struggled into his coat before opening the door. Torrents of rain bounced off the windscreen as he eased his way out of the car and approached the two disconsolate PCs looking over the bridge.

'Why have you called out Major Crimes? Surely this is just a blockage?'

The older of the two PCs looked at Bhaki with a hint of exasperation that didn't just come from having to stand in the rain. 'Have a deeks yoursel' and you'll see why.'

Bhaki leaned over the parapet and looked down at the roiling mass of water and driftwood fighting to get through the narrow arch of the bridge. Nothing looked amiss at first, but the longer he looked, the more he saw.

Stretched between two oak trees on either side of the river, a wire rope hung in the water. Looking more closely at the tree on the left bank, Bhaki saw a second, almost completely submerged, wire rope.

The twin ropes had entangled a number of trees washed down the river by the recent heavy rains, their bulky stems and branches forming a makeshift dam solidified by countless smaller pieces of driftwood caught up in their branches.

One thing Harry Evans always impressed on his team was to look for what wasn't there, missing items which were clues only by their absence.

Looking down at the trees entangled in the wire, Bhaki saw heavy branches, but no root ball protruding from the water. While the bottom part of a tree would be the heaviest end, the raging waters would soon strip away the soil encased in the root ball.

Peering harder, Bhaki spied a cleanly cut end at the bottom of a tree. The suggestions his mind was making were exhilarating yet disturbing. Raising his eyes from the torrent, he looked upstream and found a possible motive peeking between the squalls of rain.

With help from the first rays of morning light, he saw the outlines of a building. Peering with more intensity, he saw timber boards lining the gable. The front which overlooked the normally idyllic river showed huge windows rent open by river-carried flotsam. A doorway in the gable showed just three feet above the water, giving him a ready scale of the destruction.

The whole of the ground floor would be a mess of silt, twisted debris and foul water. The clean-up would take weeks, if not months, and would cost many thousands of pounds.

Bhaki's memory kicked in and he recalled a news item about the ruined building. It was to be a new restaurant. Owned by one of the county's leading chefs, its opening was anticipated with excitement by many local foodies.

Realising the seriousness of the situation for the first time, Bhaki reached for his mobile. The destruction to the restaurant was a secondary concern. The first thing to do was ensure there was no risk to civilians or animals from the rising flood water. Then there was the issue of the safety of those below the bridge to consider. If the makeshift dam was breeched or the wire rope broke, the ensuing torrent of water would cause untold destruction to properties further downstream.

Bhaki climbed into his car as DS Neil Chisholm answered his call. 'It's Amir. This shout I've just had is a bad one. Someone's created a dam at the bridge. If it gives way, there's no telling what danger it will pose to anyone living downstream.'

He paused to listen for a few seconds. 'There's two PCs here. I'll get one of them to go to a farm I can see at the end of the road. The farmer there should be able to tell them of anyone who lives in the first mile or two. The other can stop all traffic from crossing the bridge.'

Neither man mentioned Bill Barker, but each of their thoughts went to the PC who had lost his life in the floods of 2009 when a bridge he was standing on was washed away by flood water.

Listening as Chisholm spoke, Bhaki watched the rain bounce off his windscreen as it was whipped by a ferocious wind.

'The river is in a little valley, and the road is built up to create a natural dam. The only way the water can get away is to go under the bridge or swell until it comes over the road.' Bhaki wiped his forehead. 'I dare say you could get a digger in to create another route for the water to go, but to do that you'd have to dig up the road. It may be better to wait for the rain to stop and the water to drain away naturally, provided the dam holds. I'll get these PCs mobilised and call you back. Can you find out what the weather forecast is?'

Approaching the two PCs who had retreated from the centre of the bridge, Bhaki issued some instructions. The elder of the two assessed his orders with a canny gaze. 'Can you use your car to block one end of the road? I'll keep traffic away from t'other.'

Bhaki nodded as the man headed away to do his task. From the purposeful set to his stride, he suspected the man knew of a barn or building where he could shelter from the rain.

Leaving the other PC to see the farmer and alert anyone else who may be at risk, Bhaki climbed into his car and pulled out of the parking space. Building up as much speed as he could, he crossed the bridge as quickly as possible, then slammed on the brakes to negotiate a sharp corner. Reaching a small junction at the end of the road, he manoeuvred the car back and forth until it blocked the road. Walking back to the bridge with the cold rain stinging any exposed skin, he started to chew over possible motives for blocking the river.

The obvious answer was that it was someone with a grudge against the chef behind the new restaurant. Experience, however, had taught him obvious answers were correct on very few occasions.

Trying to get his mind to work as laterally as the rain, Bhaki guessed at other possibilities.

Was the real target further downstream, intended as a victim of the dam breaking? If so, who? A farmer or householder with property adjacent to the river? What about the chef? Had

*he run into money problems and sabotaged his own restaurant
for an insurance payout?*

Reaching the edge of the bridge, he looked down at the
swirling orange maelstrom once more and saw the water
roiling as it fought to find a way past the blockade. Peering at
the tree around which the wire ropes were moored, he saw no
sign of the wires.

Bhaki was filled with a further sense of dread as he realised
the water level was rising. The deeper the water got, the more
pressure would be applied to the dam and the wire ropes which
held the trees. Sooner or later, the wires would snap or one of
the trees would be uprooted. When that happened, there would
be nothing to stop the entire body of water hurtling
downstream with a cargo of hefty trees ready to bulldoze any
obstacle.

Sprinting the two hundred yards back to his car, Bhaki
thumbed his phone and called Chisholm again. As he relayed
his concerns, he saw a marked police car pull up behind his
Astra. He didn't recognise the face in the passenger seat, but
he could tell from the pips on the epaulettes that a Chief
Inspector had arrived.

Ending his call with Chisholm, Bhaki approached the
passenger side of the police car and showed his warrant card to
the Chief Inspector.

Grateful for the thumb jerked towards the back seat, he got
in, introducing himself as he did so.

'I'm Chief Inspector Ingles. What do you make of it, lad?'

Ingles had the slow drawl of East Cumbrians who'd grown
up in the countryside. While the man may now be more
familiar with the golf course than the fells, he still retained the
look of a farmer.

'It's definitely been done on purpose. The biggest question,
as far as I'm concerned, is who's supposed to be the target.
I've spoken with DS Chisholm, and he's checked out what's
downstream. Thankfully, there are no properties within a
hundred yards of the river. He's contacting the farmers below
the bridge and advising them to stay away from low-lying
fields in case the dam breaks.'

Ingles looked at Bhaki with a steady gaze. 'Well done, lad. You've covered the main points. I'll take over the situation here. You crack on with finding the toerag who did it.'

'Yes sir. Thank you, sir.' Bhaki hesitated for a moment, unsure of just how much to tell the Chief Inspector. 'I've asked DS Chisholm to start looking into any possible targets. If we're lucky, one of them will be able to point us towards the perpetrator.'

'It's a good plan, but be wary.' A crease of authority etched itself onto Ingles' face. 'The public can be too quick to point the finger so they can settle their petty scores.'

'Don't worry, sir. My DI has warned me all about that.'

'Ah yes. You're on Harry Evans' team, aren't you?' Ingles paused, compassion filling his eyes. 'How's he doing?'

'He's bearing up, sir.'

'Tell him I sent my best when you see him.'

Sensing he'd been dismissed, Bhaki walked back to his car with his thoughts centred on Harry Evans.

He'd gone round to see him with Lauren Phillips a couple of days ago. Evans had worn a brave face, but there was no disguising the pain he felt. He and Lauren had uttered meaningless platitudes while Evans had tried to be strong. Sensing the effort their presence was costing him, they'd made their excuses at the first opportunity and left him alone with his grief. They knew he appreciated their presence, even if he wasn't yet ready for it.

Returning his mind to the task at hand, Bhaki dug a pair of wellies from the back of his car and set off back to the bridge. He had a theory he wanted to check out and this was the only way to do it. Already soaked to the skin, he reckoned it was better to follow his instinct now, rather than waiting for the rain to stop. If he could confirm his suspicions, he'd be better placed when it came to drawing up a list of suspects.

The ground level was twenty feet above the river bank and the terrain was hard going until Bhaki found a worn path.

As he walked, he kept his eyes on the track, making sure he didn't catch a root or trip over a fallen bough. The last thing he wanted was to fall and roll into the river.

Stopping every fifty yards, he surveyed the bank leading down to the river. When his eyes didn't find what he was looking for, he would move on.

Three hundred yards from the road, he found what he was seeking. Right along the bank of the river was a row of tree stumps, each one bearing the reddish cream colour of freshly sawn wood.

Looking down to the river, he could see no sign of the felled trees. Whoever had cut these trees down had dropped them into the waters below. Examining the ground, he found no sign of footprints or any other clue left by the malicious woodsman.

Counting twenty-three stumps, he saw that each was a minimum of two feet in diameter, with the largest over four feet wide.

The cuts appeared to be clean and even, to his mind the work of a professional forestry worker or at least someone who knew how to use a chainsaw properly.

*   *   *   *

Bhaki walked into the office and picked up the information Chisholm had printed for him. On the typed sheets was a list of all those who owned property or livestock which may have been caught either by the rising floodwater or were at risk if the dam suffered a sudden breach.

'Is this all there is, eight possible victims?'

Chisholm's answer was cut short by Lauren's flounced entrance.

'Bloody Chief Super's just had a right go at me.' Her face was a mask of indignance as she stomped about the office. 'Says my heels are too high and that I'd never be able to chase after anyone in them.'

'He may have a point.'

'I'll say the same to you as I said to him.' Lauren's eyes burned as she rounded on Bhaki. 'I'll race you over a hundred yards for a hundred quid.'

'In those heels, you'd break an ankle after five.' Bhaki couldn't resist prodding the wasp's nest that was Lauren's commitment to high heels.

'Anytime, anyplace.'

'That's enough.' Chisholm's voice may have been raised an octave or two, but an underlying fondness shone through. Being told off by him was like a favourite uncle admonishing a gentle reprimand. 'Think yourself lucky, Amir. Only eight people to investigate. Lauren, you've got a suspicious fire at the old bakery to look into. I'd rather you did that than waste your time challenging every male in the building to a race. We all know you can run like the wind, heels or no heels. If you're not smart enough to realise the Chief Super has a problem with the way you dress, you shouldn't be a detective.'

Bhaki settled himself into his usual chair, thankful for the set of clean dry clothes he kept in his locker for days like this.

Looking at the list of names gave him no inspiration. The DS had run a basic search on each name, and none of the eight were in debt, involved in any legal disputes, or had the slightest hint of money worries.

Due to the restaurant's proximity to the bridge, the chef was the most probable target. Looking at the details Chisholm had provided, Bhaki found nothing in his past which would drive someone to such lengths. Besides, if the chef was the target, a gallon of petrol and a box of matches would have achieved the same result with a lot less hassle.

One of the farmers listed was reputed to be one of the country's top breeders of pedigree bulls. He may well have been targeted by a rival, but the more he thought about it, the less he liked the farmer as the target. While not a country person by any means, he couldn't recall seeing any cows or cattle in the fields for weeks. He guessed they must be kept in barns or sheds during the winter months. If this was true, they wouldn't be at risk from the floodwaters. Something a rival farmer would know. Again, a gallon of petrol and a box of matches would have garnered the same result.

Another factor praying on his mind was the apparent expertise the perpetrator had with a chainsaw. That pointed to a professional woodsman or forester, yet it begged the question of why they'd do something which would so obviously implicate them.

Knowing he wasn't going to find the answers from a sheet of paper, Bhaki made a couple of calls, picked up his jacket, and prepared to get soaked again.

*   *   *   *

Knocking on the door of the Giddy Goose, Bhaki was met by a worried-looking man in chef's whites.

'You the detective who called?' Ian Trent was a shadow of the person who often appeared on local news items. Without the make-up and lighting provided by TV, he looked just like any other person would when confronted with bad news, the bubbly personality replaced by a matter-of-fact acceptance, the sparkle in his eye dulled by stress, and the wild thoughts accompanying the setbacks.

Bhaki nodded. 'I need to ask you a few questions.'

Trent gestured towards the nearest table. 'Let's have a seat, yeah?'

Bhaki took a glance around as he pulled a notebook from his pocket on his way to the table. The décor of the room was ultra-modern, with clean lines and neutral tones. Splashes of colour were provided by examples of modern art hung on the walls.

'How did you hear of the flood?'

'Oliver Davies called me.'

Bhaki didn't have to ask who Davies was. A sign for his construction company had been sited at the entrance of the road to the new restaurant.

'We're looking at everyone who has been, or may be, affected by the flood. Obviously, as proprietor of the restaurant, your name is at the top of our list.'

Trent appeared to shrink in stature as he came to terms with the fact he may have been specifically targeted. 'Why would someone do such a thing to me? I haven't got any enemies, I'm fair in my business dealings and I pay my bills on time.'

'We don't know for certain who the intended target is. Can you think of anyone who may have a grudge against you?'

'No.' The answer was instinctive and delivered with conviction. 'As I said, I pay my bills on time and play fair with suppliers and customers.'

'What about professional rivals?' Bhaki hesitated, knowing his next sentence may not be well received. 'Other chefs, local restaurant owners and so on?'

Trent's head shook from side to side as he spoke. 'I seriously doubt it. I have a good relationship with them all. Tell me, how much do you know about fine dining, detective?'

'Only that I can't afford it.'

Trent's frown deepened, making Bhaki regret his flippant remark.

'Perhaps not every week, but for a special occasion?'

'I guess.' Bhaki made the concession out of good manners rather than a sense of agreement. He'd never yet had a long-term relationship, and any family occasions were always hosted in his parent's restaurant.

'There you go. Besides, I did my research before even starting this project. What I'll be offering at River View is going to be aimed at the more discerning customer. There's no place within fifty miles which will be able to compete.'

'Won't that be the problem?'

'Not at all. River View will provide a different level of food and service to anywhere in the region and will be priced accordingly.' Trent gave a wry smile. 'In short, I'm going after the posh pound and people celebrating special occasions.'

Trent's insistence of not competing with local businesses made sense on some levels, but Bhaki doubted competing restaurateurs would see it the same way. There were only so many customers available, and a new restaurant led by a chef who was fast becoming a national celebrity would impact on someone's business.

'What about suppliers you've worked with, or people from your personal life?'

'I've used the same suppliers for the ten years I've had the lease on here, and I married my school sweetheart.' A fond smile twitched at Trent's lips. 'Fifteen years married and two kids, and we still haven't had a cross word.'

'What about the people who work here with you? What will happen to them once you leave? Have you poached any staff from local restaurants?' The questions tumbled from Bhaki's mouth as fast as they entered his brain.

'I've promoted staff here so I can concentrate on River View. The new staff haven't been poached from anywhere, they've approached me personally or answered job ads I've put out. I look after my staff, and they have all been very supportive and excited about the opening.'

'Do you know anyone who is a woodsman or someone who is good with a chainsaw?'

Trent leaned back in his seat, his eyes raised to the ceiling. 'Not that I can think of. My wife gets someone in to do our garden, but I don't know his name or if he even has a chainsaw. Why do you ask?'

When Bhaki told him, the chef's face paled to a milky white.

Bhaki stood to leave and held a card out. 'If you think of anyone who may have a grudge against you or the builder, please don't hesitate to contact me.'

As he left the restaurant, Bhaki thought about the suspicions he'd had. First of all, the restaurant was the most probable target in the area. So, if Trent wasn't the target, who was?

The builder Oliver Davies may lose a few quid on materials lost, but he'd gain the extra work repairing the damage done by the flood. Davies himself may be responsible, but it was a stretch that he was desperate enough to sabotage his own work. A call to DS Chisholm would soon establish the builder's character and business dealings. After that, he could look at a certain someone else and see what he could unearth there.

*　　*　　*　　*

Bhaki pulled into the farmyard and parked between a mud-splattered pick-up and a tractor. Once out of the car, he retrieved his wellies from the boot – he'd learned the hard way about the damage a farm could do to a pair of brogues.

Not getting an answer from the farmhouse door, he started to walk through the outbuildings, the deep rumble of tractor guiding his footsteps like a homing beacon.

He found the farmer dispensing silage from a fancy trailer with a side chute. When the farmer saw him, he stopped the tractor and opened the door.

'Mr Foster?'

'Aye, that's me, lad. Who are you?' His eyes narrowed. 'I don't see reps wi'out an appointment mind.'

Bhaki explained who he was and why he was there. He watched as Foster clambered out of the tractor, the old man slow and deliberate with his movements.

'What is it you want to know, lad? I've a lot to be doing.'

Bhaki could tell the farmer's mind was a lot quicker than his aged limbs, so he cut to the chase. 'I don't know how much you've heard about the flood down by the bridge, but the blockage was done on purpose. What I want to know is who could be harmed by it and who would want to harm them?'

'There's only me owns land as is flooded, other than that fancy new restaurant. I had no sheep or cattle down there, so it's no big deal for me. I guess there'll be a few fence posts need replacing and a bit of stuff to lift off the field, but it's nowt I've not had to deal with in the past. Mind, it's never been owt like as bad as it is today.'

'So I'd be right in saying the flooded fields won't harm your business?'

'You would.' Foster spat a gob of phlegm under the tractor. 'Can't say the same for thon chef and Oliver Davies. This could cost them a right packet.'

'What about anyone downstream from the bridge? Is there anyone there who would suffer if that dam broke?'

A toothless grin etched itself onto Foster's face. 'Nah. There's no-one as would be affected by more than a few lost sheep or ruined fences.'

Bhaki called Chisholm as he returned to his car. Listening with care, he got all the details he'd asked for. As ever,

Chisholm had unearthed all the information requested and more besides.

Oliver Davies' business was on a sure footing and his accounts showed a steady flow of work and profits in line with the size of his business. There was nothing about Davies on the PND, other than a couple of speeding fines and a parking ticket.

*　　*　　*　　*

Bhaki hadn't even got out of his car when he was confronted by a man wearing sodden work-clothes and a desperate air.

'If you're another one from the press, then you can bugger off.'

Bhaki flashed his warrant card and watched as the man's expression went from anger to pleading in a heartbeat.

'I've a few questions for you, Mr Davies. Is there somewhere we can talk out of the rain?'

Davies walked towards his office by way of an answer. An open door to a shed in his yard showed a bunch of workmen half-heartedly sweeping and stacking various goods and tools.

Bhaki's heart fluttered for a moment when a workman lifted a chainsaw and carried it towards a liveried van. As the man swung it round, he saw its blade was too short to have felled the size of trees dropped into the river. Still, it showed Davies had the equipment and tools necessary.

Following Davies into the office, Bhaki saw a secretary with a phone wedged under one ear and a mass of papers stacked in neat piles on the two desks.

'This is going to ruin me. Twenty-five years I've spent building up this business, and one flood is going to ruin me.'

Bhaki measured his words before speaking, lest his racing pulse cause him to offend the distraught builder.

'What do you mean, sir?'

'I mean that I'll never be able to pay the penalty clauses on late completion. I've got over fifty grand laid out for materials and the wage bill is touching twenty-five.'

Bhaki held up his hands in apology. 'I'm sorry, but I don't understand. Can you explain how this will ruin you?' It was cruel to ask Davies to spell it out, but Bhaki knew he needed to get a proper understanding of the situation.

Davies' heavy slump into a chair told Bhaki of the pressure he was under. 'I gave Ian Trent a price of three hundred and twenty thousand to build his restaurant. It is to be paid in three instalments of a hundred grand, with twenty held back for a year as retention for any building issues which arise. The first instalment was a third of the way through, the second at two thirds and the final one is to be paid upon completion.'

Every word from Davies' mouth told of his burden, of the pressure he felt, and of how near he was to admitting defeat. His tone was subdued, every muttered word carrying its own weight in self-pity.

'Surely the final payment of a hundred thousand will cover your outlay?'

'It would, but it's not that simple. There was ten grand's worth of timber flooring waiting to be laid and the solid oak bar cost me eight grand to make. Plus there is a non-completion penalty of twenty thousand a week. By the time I replace those and then lose the money for late completion, I'll be done for.'

Bhaki just managed to keep his internal wince from showing on his face. 'Have you any idea how long it'll take to repair the water damage?'

Davies didn't lift his eyes from the desk when he answered. 'I haven't been allowed to even see the damage from the road, but from what I've heard, it'll be a couple of months at least. And that's working twelve hour days, seven days a week.'

'What about insurance? Surely your insurance will cover you?'

'They would if I'd taken any out. I do in towns and cities, where there's a good chance of having stuff nicked, but not in a place like this.'

Bhaki let his mind comprehend the scale of the builder's personal disaster while the older man shifted his gaze from the desk to the floor.

'What about Mr Trent? Won't he have insurance that will cover the building?'

Davies gave a snort. 'I spoke with him yesterday. He said he was gonna start doing all that kind of thing next week.'

'Do you think he'll hold you to the late completion penalties being as this was a malicious act that's nothing to do with your workmanship?'

'I can only hope not.' Davies glanced at his watch. 'I'm due to meet him and Chief Inspector Ingles over there in an hour. I'll know then if my business is going to survive or not.'

Bhaki brushed away the feeling of being an intruder into grief and changed his tack.

'The flooding of the restaurant was caused by a deliberate act and, to my mind, either you or Mr Trent were the intended targets. Bearing in mind what you've just told me, I'm inclined to think it was aimed at ruining you.' Bhaki changed his voice from matter-of-fact to a more gentle tone. 'Can you think of anyone who'd A, know how much you'd suffer and B, have the means and skill to cause the river to be dammed?'

A burning fire shone from Davies eyes when his head snapped up. 'You mean this all happened because some bastard is trying to ruin me? If that's true, then you better hope you find him before I do.'

Bhaki's hand shot up in a halt gesture as he matched the builder's aggressive tone. 'Stop right there. Vigilante justice isn't the answer. You've enough to deal with without getting yourself into trouble with us.'

After pausing to let his words sink in, he returned his voice to a less confrontational pitch. 'You'd be a lot better off helping us catch the person who did this and then fighting to keep your business going. Let him stew in jail while you make money. Surely that's a better punishment for him?'

Davies didn't say anything, but Bhaki could see his words were having the desired effect.

'Tell you what, if you promise to give me total co-operation, I'll do what I can to lean on Mr Trent so he doesn't hold you to the penalty clause.'

'You'd do that?'

'I will if you can tell me of anyone you think may be behind this.'

Davies slumped back into his chair and fell silent as his mind started to work.

Bhaki kept quiet and let his eyes wander around the office as he waited. He was confident Davies would make the right decision, but could tell the man needed a moment to think.

'There's two people I think could have done it, but I don't believe either would.'

'You'd be surprised what some people will do because of jealousy or because they feel a need for petty revenge. Who are they?'

'One is Frank Young, who owns Wetherington's Building Supplies in Keswick, and the other is my wife's brother, Eric. Eric Sampson.'

'Why do you think they might have done it?'

'They're the only two people I've fallen out with for years.' Bhaki raised an eyebrow. 'Frank Young threw a wobbler when I returned a whole batch of timber because it wasn't good enough for the job. He called me worse than shit, so I told him to stick his business up his arse and that I'd get materials elsewhere.'

'And your brother-in-law?'

'He blames me for my wife's death. Reckons if I'd been home to help with the kids more, she wouldn't have been so tired. She fell asleep at the wheel.' Davies' voice fell to a whisper. 'Perhaps he's right.'

Bhaki didn't know how to answer, so he didn't try.

Davies scribbled on a scrap of paper. 'That's Eric's address. He used to work in the woods, but gave it up a few years ago when his back got too bad. I dunno if he's still got his chainsaws, but I know he's capable of doing it. As for Frank, he could easily get his hands on a chainsaw and a bit of wire rope if he wanted.'

Bidding Davies a goodbye with a reminder against taking the law into his own hands, Bhaki walked back to his car with his mind whirling.

He now had two possible suspects with the means and a possible motive. The weather and the restaurant's isolated location had provided the opportunity.

*   *   *   *

Travelling towards Keswick, he pulled into a lay-by to grab a fried egg roll from a roadside burger van. While not the most nourishing of foods, it would fill a hole and let his mind concentrate on the task at hand.

The brother-in-law seemed too ideal a suspect and, if it was him, Bhaki may have a very hard time proving it. Unless there was a way chainsaw cuts could be attributed to a particular chain, it would be nigh on impossible proving an individual had committed the crime.

Finishing off the roll and wiping his hands on the paper napkin, he decided to check if Chisholm had any news for him.

Hanging up the call, he digested the information he'd just been given. Chisholm's digging into Trent's wife had unearthed a new suspect.

Deciding to follow the leads from Davies first due to the fact he was only a couple of miles from both Frank Young and Eric Sampson, he started the engine and pointed the car towards Keswick.

Visiting Wetherington's Building Supplies to see Frank Young, he found the man absent. According to his staff, he was currently holidaying in America. A quick call to Chisholm confirmed Young had been out of the country for the last week.

Parking underneath the branches of a beech tree, Bhaki examined the rows of bungalows with their neat gardens. There was a feeling of community and respect permeating the air. Residents here would be respectable citizens of a certain age.

When Eric Sampson answered his door, Bhaki's heart sank. There was no way the man before him could have felled the trees. The plaster cast on his right arm showed the discolouring synonymous with at least a fortnight's wear.

Introducing himself, Bhaki followed Sampson inside, refusing the offer of a cuppa. While Sampson himself was unable to wield a chainsaw, he may have organised others to do his dirty work.

'I'm sorry, lad, but I have no idea why you'd want to speak to me.' Sampson's eyes narrowed. 'It's nowt to do with that Mrs Hughes across the road, is it?'

'No. It's to do with your brother-in-law, Oliver Davies.'

'What's up? Is he all right?' Concern showed in his eyes. 'We've had our differences, but he's all them kids have.'

'It's nothing like that. A building site he was working on has been deliberately flooded, and we're looking for the person who did it.'

Sampson fell silent for a moment as he considered Bhaki's words. When he spoke, it was with a measured tone and intelligent insights.

'So you think that Oliver may be the target of whoever flooded the area and you're looking for anyone with a grudge against him. Therefore, you'll already know we fell out after Denise died.'

Bhaki said nothing, letting the silence grow until Sampson felt compelled to fill it.

When Sampson did speak, his voice was filled with remorse. 'I regret what I said to him at the time. Some of the words I used then were unforgivable. He was filled with grief and, like an idiot, I heaped more misery onto him in an attempt to find someone to blame. There was an inquest into the accident and it was found that the other driver was to blame. Because of my poor judgement, I didn't just lose a sister, I lost a brother-in-law and two nephews.'

'Haven't you tried to reconcile with him?' Bhaki couldn't stop the question, despite it being nothing to do with the case. Sampson's pain was all too evident and it tore at him.

'He won't speak to me and after what I said, and I don't blame him.'

'I see.' Bhaki excused himself and left Sampson to his regrets.

*   *   *   *

Having checked in with Chisholm once more, Bhaki now had the details he needed on his final suspect. Everything the DS had unearthed pointed to Richard King being the culprit. Now it was a case of building evidence against him.

Knocking on King's door got no answer. It was possible he was out on a job, but a Transit van bearing his name and the words 'Landscape Gardener' was parked askew in his driveway.

Twice more he knocked on the door, each time harder and longer. Still his knocks went unanswered. A light on from a downstairs room gave him hope someone was home, so he pressed his face against the glass to peer inside. What he saw made him run back to the front door and throw his shoulder at the lock side.

It took four attempts before his slight weight burst the lock and allowed him access to the house. Dashing into the lounge, he checked the pulse of the man lying on the couch. There was one. Faint, but there all the same.

As he recited the address to Control, with a request for an ambulance, he started to take in the clues offered by the prone man. There was no attempt at finesse with the makeshift bandage tied over the right thigh of his jeans. A large amount of blood had seeped from the wound it covered, and had soaked into the fabric of the couch. The man's bare left shoulder bore a dark bruise which showed the scratches of a glancing blow delivered by a heavy object. On the table by the couch lay a set of car keys and an empty blister pack of aspirin.

To Bhaki's mind, it looked as if King – if that was the man on the couch – had been caught by a tree he was felling and had cut his leg with his chainsaw. Patching up the wound with his shirt, he'd returned home and passed out on the couch too afraid to call an ambulance. Blood loss had drained him more than anticipated and now he was unconscious, unfeeling of his pain.

Aware he had a perfect opportunity to do a bit of unofficial snooping, Bhaki went into the man's office. The computer was on and when he moved the mouse, he found a number of folders on the desktop. Most bore the usual records expected of any business, but three had women's names as their titles. One of those names was Fiona Trent.

Clicking on the folder, Bhaki was met with a two other folders, one titled 'Pictures', the other 'Correspondence'.

Clicking on the pictures one first, he found a lot of pictures of Fiona Trent which appeared to have been taken without her knowledge. Some of the pictures showed her with her husband at various functions.

Checking the other folder, he found emails between Fiona and King. Scanning through them, he found the first email from Fiona stating her husband was too busy to take care of their garden and she needed to hire a landscape gardener.

Realising what had happened, Bhaki tried the other folders bearing female names and at first found them to be similar to Fiona Trent's. Yet when he looked at the correspondence folders, he saw King's replies had gone from businesslike to flirty before becoming professions of love. Both women had turned him down flat and had severed all contact.

As paramedics entered the house, Bhaki saw the whole picture. Obsessed with Fiona Trent, King had flooded the restaurant in an attempt to keep her husband busy. No doubt he'd planned to make a play for her affections at some point in the near future.

Final Days

John Campbell pushed the sheaf of papers into a file and added it to the growing pile on the right hand side of his desk. Today was his last day as a Detective Inspector for Police Scotland. All things being well, he planned to coast through the day finalising paperwork and completing his research on the team he'd be taking over.

'Guv?' DC Anderson's head poked round the faded door casing. 'We've got a shout and Bawbag says he wants you to lead.'

Campbell kept the grumble to himself. It was typical of DCI Colin 'Bawbag' Venters to thrust a case on him on his last day. Venters was a ladder-climber whose next promotion was his only concern. Robotic in his understanding of human emotions, he had tried to make Anderson work a back shift the day she'd buried her mother. In a former life, he would have been the one whipping pyramid-building slaves.

'What's the shout?'

'Marie Mason is saying she's been raped.' Anderson's expression answered his next five questions.

Marie Mason was a familiar name to the whole team. She'd made regular claims and allegations against persons known and unknown to her. An attention-seeker of the highest order, she had allegedly been raped six times, indecently assaulted a dozen and had filed more than a hundred complaints about a neighbour she thought was spying on her. Not once had a conviction been brought against any of her claimed aggressors.

About a year ago, her calls to the police had stopped, prompting bad-taste jokes about her having died.

'She's been too quiet for too long. Who's she pointing the finger at this time, the neighbour?'

A shrug. 'I dunno. She called the station direct, said she'd been raped, gave her address and then hung up.'

'If Bawbag wants us to respond, then we'll respond.' Campbell lifted a couple of files from his desk. At this time of day, it would take at least twenty minutes to get to Marie's tenement flat. He could do a spot of reading on the way.

As Anderson drove along the traffic-filled streets, he turned the volume of the car's radio to a muted background level. Irony was in full flow today, as the first song he recognised was A-ha's 'Cry Wolf'.

Chancellor Street was crowded with parked cars and vans bearing the names of a construction firm. Workmen were trailing in and out of a property shrouded with a large scaffold. Crisp new windows were being carried in as old ones were being hauled out and thrown into one of the three skips arranged haphazardly by the kerb.

Walking along to Marie's address, Campbell lifted his eyes to the buildings and soaked in the sight of the sandstone frontages. Bathed in sunshine, the once proud buildings looked downtrodden and depressed. Decades of grime and pollution soiled their faces, sullying them in a way that was absorbed by their inhabitants.

Those who lived in these tenements were strong people whose iron constitutions were rusted by bad diets, bigotry and alcohol dependence, their life aspirations nothing more than a week in Blackpool, an Old Firm win, or the next bottle of Buckfast.

Campbell knocked on the door with resignation, expecting tears and the usual unfounded allegations.

It was a few years since Marie had last filed a rape allegation. Even she would have to admit that anyone raping her was a bit of a stretch. Standing five foot high and three wide, Marie Mason wasn't your typical rape victim. Pulling sixty, she was a hard woman chiselled into a gargoyle by an unrelenting life of disappointment.

When the door opened, he couldn't stop the gasp of amazement escaping his pursed lips.

Marie's face was a mass of bruised tissue and fresh cuts. One eye was swollen closed and beginning to show the first signs of discolouration. Her nose was squashed flat and a trickle of blood from each corner of her mouth gave her a pair of red fangs.

Her one good eye sparked in recognition. 'Good. An Inspector.'

Campbell followed the shuffling woman into her home. Like Marie, the tenement displayed the marks of a vicious attack. Magazines littered the threadbare carpet, chairs were overturned and smashed crockery littered the floor of the kitchen.

In keeping with every other Glaswegian woman of her years, Marie Mason took a perverse pride in keeping her home tidy and clean. She may not have a pot to piss in, but what she did have, she kept spotless.

What surprised him was the plasma TV thrown onto the floor and the boot-print covered remains of a laptop. He could only surmise that, like so many others in city, she would be in line for a loyalty card at the black market.

Every instinct Campbell possessed as a copper told him Marie's latest claim was, for once, genuine. Yet he'd been tricked before by people injuring themselves to play the role of victim.

'Can you tell us what happened?' Campbell righted a chair for Marie and squatted down on his haunches so as not to tower over her.

'I answered the door and this ugly bastard shoved me. I tried to push him back, but he was too big. Fucker hit me a few times and then pulled me onto the bed.' A look of shame washed over her face before a look of determination replaced it. 'Bastard pulled my skirt up and my knickers down.'

Marie's telling of her rape was matter-of-fact. She delivered details with the conviction of certainty.

Campbell took down the details while Anderson called for an ambulance and a rape consultant.

When Marie finished, Campbell had what he thought was enough information to identify her alleged rapist.

'Marie, I have a question for you.' He swallowed. 'You're not going to like it, but in light of every other claim you've made I have to ask it.'

'Whit is it son?'

'Are you sure this really happened? Because if we have you examined by a doctor and she says you haven't been raped, then you will be given a bill for the doctor's time.' Campbell spread his hands wide. 'It's the way things have to be done with all the budget cuts we've had.'

Marie levelled her gaze until she met his eyes with a fierce one-eyed stare. 'Get the doctor son. I'll no' be getting any bill.'

Campbell's lie had given him the information he needed. People like Marie lived in fear of another bill. There was no way she would risk having to pay a penny because of a fabrication. Therefore the rape was genuine.

A paramedic arrived and escorted Marie downstairs to the ambulance as the CSI team arrived.

Leaving them to do their jobs, Campbell rounded up Anderson and began knocking on neighbouring doors.

Of the five other doors in the building, only one yielded an answer.

The man who answered carried a few days worth of beard growth, a visible hangover, and breath rank enough to fell an elephant. Campbell threw a few questions at the man, but the answers slurred back at him were of no help.

After summoning a couple of DCs to do a more thorough job of the door-to-doors, Campbell and Anderson set off back to the station.

They hadn't driven a hundred yards before his nose was back in the file on Harry Evans.

The man he was due to replace was everything he wasn't, a rule-breaker who followed gut-instinct rather than procedure. He knew the type only too well. His first DI had been just like Evans, coarse, unruly, and almost impossible to work for. His ways had been stuck in a time when confessions were extracted with a closed fist or the threat of being held responsible for every unsolved crime since Cain killed Abel.

The team backing Evans up all showed decent qualities, but they, too, had a history of renegade ways. He would need to exert his authority from day one and stamp out any inclination to disregard the rule book.

'I said, what do you think about Marie's story?'

'Sorry.' Campbell brought his mind back to the case at hand. 'I think it's genuine, but you never know with her.'

'I heard what you said about the doctor. That was a clever test.'

'Thanks. I want you to drop me off at the station and then head over to the CCTV control rooms. Marie was specific about the time her rapist arrived. If she's telling the truth, you should be able to pinpoint him pretty easily.'

'OK.' Anderson's voice wasn't filled with enthusiasm for the task. 'Do you think we'll get lucky?'

'You never know. There's cameras there, so we might.'

*　*　*　*

Reaching the station, Campbell grabbed a coffee and a bacon roll from the canteen and headed back to his desk. Until he heard from the doctor, the Crime Scene Manager, or Anderson, there was little he could do to progress the case.

He was looking forward to his transfer to the Major Crimes team at Carlisle. Not only would it provide a fresh challenge, it would remove the hour-and-a-half commute he faced at each end of his shifts. Living in Gretna and transferring to a more local force had been his new wife's idea. Sarah hadn't wanted to leave her hometown for Glasgow, and he'd had his fill of policing a city inhabited by bampots, neds and gangs intent on preserving a hold on their territory.

It had taken a year for the right transfer to come along, but when it did, he applied that very day. It had been a fraught process, almost thwarted by the one black mark in his career, but the planets aligned and his transfer went through.

Now everything in his life was perfect. A new wife, a baby due within the month, and a new challenge just fifteen minutes from home. He'd even made a twelve grand profit on the house he'd sold when moving to Gretna.

He shuffled paper for a half-hour before his phone rang. It was the Crime Scene Manager with a preliminary report.

The CSI team had given the flat a cursory sweep, in line with the guidelines on the extent of detail to be searched for.

Modern policing was about accounting for budget, managing resources and following the most probable leads.

The CSM wanted to know how many of the dozens of samples he was supposed to analyse. Flipping a mental coin, Campbell made his decision and asked for all the hair samples to be tested. Other forensic samples could be tested at a later date if necessary. The most telling samples would come from the doctor who examined Marie. In rape cases, there was almost always transference of hair or skin caught under the victim's nails.

It was this evidence on which most rape cases were tried.

Hanging up the phone, Campbell's mind returned to Marie and her behaviour at the tenement. Like the hypochondriac who has 'I told you I was ill' engraved onto their gravestone, there was a triumphant satisfaction about her. After all those false calls, she now had a genuine reason to make a complaint.

The physical invasion had been shrugged off with typical Glasgow fortitude. 'Ah'm jist glad his tadger was nae bigger'n his thumb.'

This time when the phone rang it was the doctor who'd examined Marie. Every word she'd spoken about her ordeal was backed up by the doctor's examination.

Marie Mason had, as claimed, been raped both vaginally and anally. The verification of her claim kicked the investigation up a gear. Her track record had meant Campbell's initial steps had been tempered with cynicism. The last thing he wanted to do on his last day was be tricked by a serial hoaxer. Now the brakes were off, he could throw extra manpower and resources at the case.

Calling the CSM, he informed him of the samples collected from the doctor. Next he called the DCs canvassing the area where Marie lived and urged them to leave no door un-knocked.

As he finished that call, Anderson rang him with excitement filling her voice. Hearing her news, he instructed her to come back and collect him.

While he waited, Campbell booted up his computer and started a search. Five minutes later, he had the information he needed and was striding down to the car park ready for Anderson's return.

* * * *

Drumming his fingers on the dashboard, Campbell felt the thrill of the chase kicking in. Just three hours ago, he was shuffling paper. Now he was on his way to arrest a potential rapist. Moments like these were the reason he loved his job.

This was the meat of the daily sandwich, and he wondered what kind of man he was going to confront. Marie Mason was nobody's idea of a desirable woman even before she'd been assaulted. It would take a special kind of twisted deviant to find her sexually attractive enough to rape.

It hadn't needed fantastic detection to follow this lead. Marie's description of her rapist and the time of her assault had given them a solid clue. CCTV cameras had shown a man in his fifties entering her tenement building at the prescribed time. After that, it was a matter of waiting until the man came out and tracking him. Like so many criminals in the city, he wasn't the sharpest knife in the drawer. He'd walked out of the door, taken twenty paces along the street, and climbed into a dirty Mondeo. A little bit of a zoom on the image had brought up the number plate in clear definition.

Baillieston was one of Glasgow's middle-ground areas. The people who lived in this area were solid working-class. Imbued with a work ethic passed down through genetics, they were the people whose hard graft kept the city running. None of their jobs could be considered a profession, but they all had aspirations for their children to do better than themselves.

Anderson pulled in behind the Mondeo from the CCTV tape. The house it was parked outside had small patch of neatly-cut grass.

It was a new build, as was every other house on the street. White and red brick boxes topped with brown tiles and finished with plastic, where once timber would have been used.

While each house looked presentable enough, the conformity would have driven Campbell insane. The entire street was the same, like a row of soldiers standing to attention. Campbell guessed the architect got bored after the first house and just copied and pasted the rest of the street so he could make his tee time.

'Let's do this.' Campbell strode to the door, fingering the collapsible baton in his pocket.

The door opened to reveal a woman in her fifties. Well presented, she had a toddler on her hip that looked at Campbell with innocent eyes. 'Can I help you?'

'DI Campbell. I'm looking for Bill Osbourne.'

Concern hit the woman's face in an instant. 'Is it our Vicky? Is she OK? Please tell me she's OK.'

Campbell softened his face, wondering who Vicky was. 'It's not about Vicky. Is Mr Osbourne here?'

'He's in the back garden.' The woman turned to the child with a relieved smile. 'Do you hear that Chelsea? Mummy's okay.'

'May we?' Campbell gestured through the house.

'Of course.'

The worry on the woman's face had been replaced with puzzlement. Now she knew her daughter was safe, she'd be expecting something juicy to discuss over the garden fence or down the bingo. Being the prime source of a new piece of gossip would raise her status for a few days.

Campbell felt a pang of pity and guilt. It wasn't just the victims who suffered. The lives of the perpetrator's family members always changed when a loved one was convicted. The more horrific the crime, the deeper the societal backlash would be.

First it would be shaming looks and turned shoulders. These would be replaced with pointed fingers and insults. Depending on the crime, the final steps could range from ostracism to graffiti and broken windows.

Osbourne's wife led them along the hallway, into the kitchen, and out of a back door into the small garden. A man was trimming a rose bush with a pair of secateurs.

Before Campbell could speak, Mrs Osbourne called out to her husband. 'Bill, there's an Inspector here to see you.'

The man's head snapped round. Fear and guilt decorated his eyes before he recovered his composure. His hands moved to remove the gardening gloves he wore, but stopped.

Campbell flicked his eyes at Anderson, who gave a short nod to confirm Osbourne was the man captured by the CCTV. 'Can we talk inside?'

It was a favoured tactic of Campbell's. Suspects would often reveal more in the comfort of their own homes than they would if hauled down to the station and interviewed on record. Once admissions had been made, an arrest would follow, and the whole process would be repeated in the interview room with its cameras and recording equipment, the formal interview simplified by the knowledge gathered in the comfortable setting.

Osbourne's wife caught the seriousness of the situation for the first time. 'Bill? What's wrong? Why do they want to talk to you?'

'Leave it, Annie.'

They followed Osbourne into the kitchen, where Annie fussed around offering cups of tea.

Osbourne dismissed her. 'Away upstairs, hen. I'll deal with their questions.'

When she left the room, he half sat against the kitchen table.

Anderson started things off. 'Can you account for your whereabouts this morning, Mr Osbourne?'

'I went to get a new pair of secateurs at Dobbies. Other than that, I've been at home.'

Campbell held back the smile from his lips at the rehearsed lie.

'So you didn't visit Chancellor Street?'

A shake of the head. 'I'm not even sure where that is.'

Anderson pressed forward. 'It's where Marie Mason lives.'

'Who?'

Campbell stepped into the conversation. 'She's a woman who was raped this morning.'

'What's that got to do wi' me?'

'The description she gave of her rapist matches you. You were caught by CCTV coming out of her house and climbing into a car. The car is registered to your name at this address.'

Osbourne's eyes flicked to the door his wife had left through. When he spoke, his voice was restrained to the barest whisper as he looked at Campbell. 'I've a wee piece down there. I slipped along to see her while the wife was getting Chelsea dressed.' A shrug accompanied his words while his expression was set to 'we're all men of the world'.

Campbell looked him up and down, making a point to focus on his still-gloved hands and the tattoos on his bare arms.

'So you don't know Marie Mason, then?'

'Definitely not.'

'That's odd, because you bear an uncanny resemblance to the description she gave of her attacker.'

'I do?' Osbourne's question was a bluff and everyone in the room knew it.

Campbell moved in for the kill. 'DC Anderson, can you remind me point-by-point the description Miss Mason gave of her attacker?'

'A mole on the right cheek.'

'Check.' Campbell pointed at Osbourne's mole.

'A bald head.'

'Check.'

Osbourne tried to dismiss their evidence. 'Lots of people have a bald head and a mole on their cheek.'

'Silver moustache.'

'Check.'

'Still not uncommon.'

'A Rangers crest tattooed on the right forearm and the name 'Vicky' tattooed on the inside of the left forearm.'

'Check and check. Would you take off your gloves please, Mr Osbourne?'

Osbourne hesitated, but capitulated under Campbell's stare. One by one, he pulled his gloves off with an obvious reluctance.

Campbell tried, without success, to keep the smile out of his voice when he spoke. 'You have marks on your right hand synonymous with having punched someone, Mr Osbourne.

Coupled with the fact you were recorded on camera entering the building where Miss Mason lives, and the fact you are a perfect fit for the description she gave of her rapist and attacker, I'm left with no choice but to arrest you for the rape and assault of one Marie Mason.'

Campbell read Osbourne his full rights, before pulling a pair of handcuffs from his pocket.

'There's just one thing I don't understand, Mr Osbourne. Why?'

What little bravado was left in Osbourne drained away as he contemplated the trouble he was in. When he spoke, it was with the self-pity of the wronged, the victim harmed by life's injustices.

'I wanted to make her pay for what she's done to my little girl. My Vicky had just turned eighteen when she got hooked on the shite that woman sells. Now she's a junkie who sucks cocks just to get enough money to buy her next fix. For the last two years she's been whoring herself to anyone in possession of a few quid and a hard-on. Every penny she makes goes to that evil bitch. She hasn't seen Chelsea since she was six months old and the way she's going, we'll be burying her before long.'

Campbell stayed quiet, waiting until Osbourne was ready to continue with his explanation. 'I wanted that bitch to see what it was like to be shagged by someone she didn't want to shag. I needed to show her what my little girl has to endure to feed her habit.'

'So you forced yourself on her?'

'Damn straight, I did. I even popped a Viagra to make sure I was up to fucking the evil bitch.'

Campbell's heart went out to the man. Osbourne's worry and grief for his daughter's plight had driven him to seek revenge of the basest kind. When his story was retold in court, he would be deprived of his freedom, as the justice system added further insult to an already grievous injury.

Campbell led a disconsolate Osbourne out to the car while Anderson placated a distraught Annie.

As soon as the wheels of the car started turning, Campbell put a call into the CSM who'd been at Marie's flat. Not getting the information he was hoping for, he called the station and issued a terse set of instructions to the Duty Sergeant.

*   *   *   *

With Osbourne deposited in a cell until the results of the forensic tests came back, there was time to kill before interviewing him. Postponing the paperwork, Campbell was the first through Marie Mason's door, a warrant in his hand.

The shock on her face when she read the warrant wasn't deep enough to hide the fear in her eyes.

Her protestations of innocence had the ring of falsehood as she tried to bluff her way out of trouble.

'Marie.' Campbell held her eye with a stern gaze as he jerked a thumb over his shoulder. 'These guys can tear your home apart looking for the stash of drugs we all know you have, or you can save us the trouble and tell us where to find them. Because, believe you me, we will find them.'

Campbell watched as Marie's good eye passed from one determined PC to another, each armed with a wrecking bar or some other tool which could be used to dismantle anything they wanted to look behind, inside or under.

While it wasn't her house they'd be wrecking, it was her home. When her landlord learned of the mess they'd make, she'd be evicted. Homeless, until a kindly judge gave her a new home. A home that was eight feet by twelve, with barred windows.

'Well?'

A sigh forced its way through pursed lips. 'There's a loose floorboard under the bed.'

Two of the PCs brushed past Campbell as they went to investigate. A minute later, they returned with a paper bag in each hand. Looking into the bags, Campbell saw wraps, pills and small blocks of dope.

'And the money?'

'The money?'

'Yes, Marie, the money.' Campbell waved a hand at her belongings. 'I can see you haven't spent much of the money you've made, so I ask again, where have you stashed it?'

Defiance leaked from Marie for the second time in as many minutes. Lifting a seat cushion from an armchair, she pushed her hand through a tear in the fabric into the bowels of the chair and pulled out a carrier bag. Bundles of twenty pound notes showed through the thin plastic walls.

'You happy?'

Campbell shook his head and started to speak the formal words of arrest.

When Marie was taken away, he stood in the centre of the room and looked around with sadness and understanding. It was little wonder Marie had sought attention and turned to selling drugs as a way to try and escape this life.

* * * *

Anderson pushed her way through the crowd and placed another pint and a whisky chaser in front of Campbell. Changed from her usual attire of business suit into a skirt and top, with her hair freed of its usual ponytail and in a carefree wave, she looked totally different.

Campbell had always been aware she was pretty, but seeing her tonight, he realised she had made the transformation from caterpillar into butterfly. The rest of the team would forever see her in a new light.

Jokes and war stories littered the air as the team gave Campbell the traditional boozy send off.

The afternoon had been spent extracting a formal confession from Osbourne and attempting to coerce Marie Mason into giving up the name of her supplier. Their fifty percent success rate was about normal. A canny old bird like Marie knew she had more to fear from her supplier than she did from the judge.

'What do you reckon to her, but?'

Campbell turned to face DS McKay, his response already guarded. 'She's a good detective. I'll bet she'll be sitting her Sergeant's exams in a year.'

'I know all that. I'm on about how hot she looks all of a sudden, but.'

McKay's use of the word 'but' as an end to every sentence was a local trait which Campbell had worked hard to rid from his own voice. It grated on him when he heard it from fellow officers.

The lecherous intention fuelling McKay's comments about a junior officer's appearance didn't sit well with him.

Resisting the urge to tell McKay where to get off, he looked him in the eye. 'And your point is?'

'Come on, big man, you know the score. She's never been seen in owt but a suit before and suddenly, at your leaving party, she's dolled up to the nines. She's after someone, and I reckon it's you, but.'

'The drink's addled your brain. I'm a married man and she'll never see me again.'

McKay's laugh echoed round the crowded bar. 'You're the one who's no' thinking straight. Tonight's her last chance for a spot of no-strings-attached fun with the DI who she follows round like a lost puppy.'

'Piss off ya numptie.' Campbell walked away to join a discussion about Celtic's forthcoming match.

Try as he might, he couldn't shake McKay's words from his mind. If the man was right, there would be worse fates than a few hours in Anderson's bed.

Once upon a time, he would have tried to snake her as a matter of habit. Now, with Sarah carrying a ring on her finger and a baby in her stomach, it was time to play the game and resist temptation. It was one thing risking a short-term relationship for a chance encounter, but to risk a marriage and face years of being a weekend dad was too great a gamble.

Strengthened by his decision, he laughed and joked with the team as they went from pub to pub. As the night wore on, other faces from the station appeared and some of the earlier starters left, conscious of the fact they were on shift the next day.

Anderson's continued presence at his elbow made Campbell start to believe McKay's suggestion. Hearing her say she was leaving was a welcome relief. Now there was no reason to fear a lack of willpower followed by a guilt trip.

When the suggestion of heading to a club was mooted, Campbell ducked out of a side door and clambered into a taxi. When the send-off had been organised, he'd booked a room in the Premier Inn at Buchanan Galleries. He could sleep the drink off before tackling the drive home. With luck, he'd be able to spend a couple of hours with Sarah before attending the briefing on the role he was due to assume next week.

He told the driver where to go and settled into the seat, thinking about his years spent policing Glasgow, the murders, rapes and gang wars more prominent in his memory than the pettier crimes. The victims and their families cascaded through his mind like some kind of photo-fit slideshow.

Climbing out of the taxi, he noticed a familiar face sitting at the bus stop outside the Premier Inn.

'Hello, guv.'

'Hi. What you doing here?'

Campbell didn't need his question answered. There was only one reason DC Hannah Anderson was here.

She stepped forward, until she was only a foot away from him, her body language removing the need for speech.

'I'm here to say goodbye to you.' As soon as the words left her mouth, she pressed her lips against his.

All thoughts of Sarah and the baby she was carrying evacuated Campbell's mind as she thrust a viperous tongue into his mouth. Feeling his body respond to her close embrace, he pulled her tighter against him.

It was Hannah who broke away from the kiss first. Stepping a half pace back, she took his hand in hers and nodded towards the Premier Inn. 'Let's move this inside.'

Hands fumbled under clothing as the lift clambered its way upwards. Reaching his room door, Campbell fished in his pockets for the key card. When he pulled it out he had a flash of premonition and turned to face Hannah.

'I'm sorry. I really want to do this, but I can't. I'm married and about to become a father.'

Hannah's face dropped as she realised his decency had thwarted her plans. When she spoke, her voice was touched with more than a tinge of bitterness. 'Bloody typical. The thing that most attracts me to you is the thing that stops us from being together.'

'I'm sorry.' Campbell reached for the door handle, knowing he had to get rid of her before he changed his mind again.

'Goodnight, guv.'

As Hannah turned and made her way towards the lift, Campbell eased the door open and went straight into the ensuite bathroom. Stripping naked, he tried to decide between an ardour-damping cold shower or a hot one coupled with a spot of self-relief.

Figuring he'd already crossed too far over the line, he twisted the shower controls to blue and prepared himself for the icy water.

A DI Harry Evans Novel
ISBN: 978-1-907565-90-8